U0165862

B2B | 業務篇

企業
英語會話

—— 李純白・著 ——

Speaking like a true B2B Sales Pro

五南圖書出版公司 印行

Preface 推薦序 1

　　這本書教您用最簡單的英語跟國外客戶談生意，也教您用最文雅的英語跟國外的供應商殺價。

　　用英語跟國外客戶談生意，其實是大部分上班族學英語的終極目標。因為許多上班族努力學英語，目的就是想要找一份薪水比較高的工作，而企業之所以願意花高薪聘請英語比較好的員工，目的就是希望員工能直接用英語跟外國人談生意。

　　然而，許多的上班族雖然對自身的業務十分熟悉，也學過許多年的英語，但是在面對國外客戶或是供應商的時候說不出話來。舉例來說，所有的業務人員都知道報價有多麼的重要，但是卻有許多業務人員不知道「報價」的英語怎麼說？而就算知道了，也往往不知道要怎麼很自然地、主動地向客戶提起報價的事情。

　　再舉個例子來說，所有的採購人員都知道殺價的重要性，但是許多亞洲的採購人員面對國外供應商的時候，卻會吞吞吐吐的說不出話來。因為我們以前在學校學的都是客客氣氣的英語，開口閉口都是「請」、「謝謝」、「對不起」，但是我們在面對國外供應商的時候，總不能這樣溫良恭儉讓吧？

　　目前市面上的商業英語書籍，大多是由英語老師所編寫的，文辭雖然優美，但往往不切實際，一件簡單的事情說的翻來覆去的，卻說不到重點；教材中教了很多複雜的文法句型跟新字彙，但是卻沒有涵蓋國際商務上最常用的一些術語。

李純白老師是我在臺大棒球隊的學長，他從臺大商學系畢業之後，遠赴美國德拉瓦大學取得 MBA 學位，學有專精，英語非常好，又曾經在跨國公司工作過二十幾年，累積了非常豐富的國際貿易與跨國管理經驗。他寫的這個系列，就是一套專為亞洲人設計的商業英語教材，這套教材避開了艱深難懂的文法句型、不用偏僻冷門的字彙，教您在短時間之內，用最簡單但也最實用英語跟國外的客戶談生意、用最文雅但是強硬的英語跟國外供應商殺價。

　　這個系列原先是以線上教材的形式推出的，結合了我們公司的 MyET 英語學習平臺，讓學生們可以藉由聽跟說的方式，迅速地掌握商業英語的核心能力。而由於這套教材非常的實用，因此在短短的一年之間，已經有十幾家臺灣、中國大陸，以及日本的大學及企業集體採購使用。而這些企業及大學，也一再跟我們反應，希望能有一套相對應的紙本書籍，對教材中的字彙文法做更詳細的解釋、對各種句型的使用時機做更深入的說明。

　　這是一套內行人為專業的商務人士所寫的英語教材，相信您一定會喜歡。

林宣敬

艾爾科技股份有限公司執行長

Preface 推薦序2

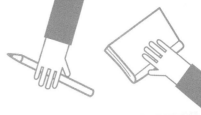

　　在世界地球村的今日，跨國的貿易和商業往來也日益頻繁，對商業大學的同學而言，掌握和駕馭商業交易的英語會話實在非常重要。感謝李純白老師能編寫此一本實用的好書，同學們如能好好研讀，當可大幅提升自己的商用英文的程度。

張瑞雄

國立臺北商業大學校長

2014年8月

Being successful in building profitable and long term B2B relationships depends on building trust, and this does not happen overnight – it takes a diligent, thorough and professional approach, underpinned by a whole lot of hard work.

想要成功建立長期又能獲利的 B2B 買賣關係，勢必得由建立互信開始。然而 B2B 互信絕非一蹴可幾，得依靠一套結合勤奮不息、周密思考、與高度專業素養為一體的工作方法。

This exact approach was so powerfully demonstrated to me when I first started working with Paul, at a time when he was being challenged with the need to build brand value in the highly competitive Taiwan market. The approach worked, and Paul earned the trust and the respect of the customers and the suppliers.

當我初開始和 Paul 共事時，就強烈感受到這種工作方法的動力。當時，Paul 接下在高度競爭的台灣市場中，建立世界級品牌價值的挑戰。幾年下來，這套方法果真奏效，Paul 贏得客戶與供應廠商共同的尊敬與信任。

Communication between West and East is not as easy as may often be assumed these days – there are many cases where

misunderstandings have led to missed opportunities – damaging that trust that is so hard to build. This has not happened in the markets handled by Paul, and again it is fitting that his careful approach is explained in these books for the benefit of others. After all, there is nothing to be gained by re-inventing the wheel, and we can all learn from the experiences of others.

如今東西方之間的溝通並不如我們想像那般容易，一個小小誤解往往就導致喪失大商機。更糟糕的是，還可能危害到辛苦建立起來的互信。然而在Paul所負責的市場裡都未曾發生過這種情況。在這一套書裡，Paul 也詳細說明了上述的工作方法，希望能帶給他人更直接的利益。畢竟很多事情不需非得自行鑽研，我們隨時能夠從別人經驗中吸取到寶貴的現成方法。

In a typically practical manner, this series of books delivers guidance that is based on real life situations and current day conditions. It is entirely logical that students of his work therefore have the opportunity to benefit from his vast array of experience and wisdom, gained at the "coal face"; the "front line"; the "sharp end" through learning and using English.

在這一套書中，Paul 以一種專業又實用的著作方式，依據各種實際的經歷，配合當今的情況，提供專業意見給使用者參考。如此一來，我相信使用這套書的讀者，能從 Paul 親身在第一線作戰所累積的黑手實務經驗與企業智慧，透過英語的練習，獲得各種企業專業技能。

Andy Royal
Managing Director
Aero Sense Technologies
http://www.aerosensetech.com/index.html

Preface 作者序

　　我自幼就對英文有興趣。最早的記憶是學齡前總愛在空白紙上胡亂塗鴉些誰也看不懂的連體字形,母親因此來問我在寫些甚麼?我回應說:英文字啊!因為當時母親在聽廣播自學英文,家裡總能找到英文教材。耳濡目染之下,喜歡學習英文的興趣不知不覺陪我走過半個世紀。

　　成長於戰後時期,很自然的在上了初中(北市仁愛初中)之後,才開始接觸正規英文教育。初中有幸受教於三位十分出色的英文老師,讓我打下扎實的基礎。高中(北市成功中學)兩位英文老師,更用另類教法延續了我學習英語的熱情。而大一(台灣大學)遇見周樹華老師,則讓我見識到年輕優秀英文老師的實力和魅力。英文之所以能一路陪伴、協助我走過人生最精采的35年,實在要感謝這些良師們的引領及教導。

　　開心順手(口)使用英文是一回事,會想動手寫英語學習的書,又是另一回事,這全是機緣。2012年中偶然在閒聊之間,和學弟林宜敬(艾爾科技創辦人)有了合作開發自學英語數位教材的想法。藉由這機緣,讓我能將35年 B2B 職涯的專業與經驗,結合我的興趣,轉換成一套適合當今企業內部英語訓練使用的教材,短短半年間,完成了 MyET 的 MBA English 教材編寫。在數位教材上市後,進一步增加內容深度與廣度,完成了這套印刷版 B2B 企業英語訓練教材。擴編的

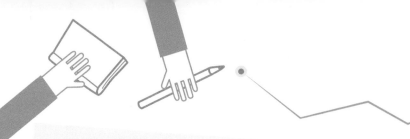

內容讓我能更貼近產業現狀，利用英語對話方式呈現企業內各部門對外溝通的情境，幫助使用者學到更實用的會話與寫作。

本系列書籍內容分成三本，分別是業務（Sales）、行銷（Marketing）、與作業研發（Operations and R&D）。這幾大部門，也是國內製造業裡，最經常使用英文對外聯繫的單位。內容編寫方式，是依據這四大部門對內對外的運作流程（業務），或者針對特定議題及情境（行銷與作業研發），以會話為主軸，輔以字彙、文法、及句型的解釋與示範。希望能利用工作的相似性，引起使用者的共鳴，自然的反覆練習，進而融會貫通並靈活運用在自身的工作上。

學習語言絕無捷徑，選對方法事半功倍。希望藉由貼近產業實務的編寫方式，讓英語學習變得更輕鬆、更自在。

特別感謝雙親，岳父母和家人的支持，尤其是在美國工作的女兒提供許多寶貴建議。感謝遠在英國的好同事 Andy Royal 專業指正，好友陳少君（Paul Chen）、蕭行志、艾爾科技林宜敬、屏東大學施百俊老師以及眾多讀者和五南出版大力支持，在這本業務篇一版後第三年頭能推出二版，讓我能適時進行修正除錯，希望能以更正確完整的內容回饋更多產業朋友。

李純白

Contents 目錄

Lesson ① 預約洽商
Making An Appointment

課文重點① Summary 1

This is an easy case in which an appointment is made as planned. While trying to make an appointment, it is essential that the salesperson offers at least two specific time options instead of simply asking the availability of the customer.

這是一次極為順利的預約拜訪對話。重點在於業務人員得主動提出至少兩個拜訪時間，讓客戶能核對其既有行程來做選擇，而不是只問客戶何時有空。

預約洽商 1　Making An Appointment 1 1-1

> **Steve** 😊：**Account Manager, Adventure Computer** 客戶經理
>
> **Cindy** 😊：**PM, MIB Electronics** 專案經理

Steve 😊：Hi Cindy, this is Steve Weeks from Adventure Computer. <u>Are you free to talk now?</u>

嗨 Cindy，我是 Adventure Computer 的 Steve Weeks，妳現在方便說話嗎？

Cindy 😊：Yes, Steve. <u>How's it going?</u>

可以呀！Steve，你好嗎？

Steve 😊：Pretty good. Regarding Project Sun, <u>I'd like to</u> meet up with you to discuss the details. <u>Is</u> Wednesday morning or Thursday afternoon <u>OK with you?</u>

我很好。我想和妳討論 Sun 專案細節。妳星期三上午或星期四下午方便嗎？

Cindy 😊：<u>Hold on a second,</u> let me check first. OK, Wednesday morning, 9:30 in my office.

你等會兒，我查一下。好，那就星期三上午 9:30 在我辦公室。

Steve 😊：Great, I'll see you then. Thank you.

好呀！到時見，謝謝妳。

Cindy： No problem, see you then.
沒問題，到時見。

❶ **essential**：必要的、必需的

It is essential to arrive on time when you visit a customer.
拜訪客戶時，一定要準時。

❷ **offer**：提出、提供

Two models of their ultrasonic cleaning machines were offered to us for selection.
他們提供二種超音波清洗機給我們選擇。

❸ **at least**：最少、起碼

As a team member, you have to at least achieve your personal sales target.
身為業務團隊的一份子，你起碼得達成自己個人的業務目標。

❹ **option**：選項、選擇

It seems that we don't have any options but match the competition.
看來我們沒有其他選擇，只能跟進。

❺ **instead of**：而不是

You should tell your boss to take action quicker instead of pushing us for orders.
你應該告訴你老闆快點採取行動，而不是一直催我們下單。

NOTE

⑥ simply：僅僅、只是

What they did was simply destroying the market. Nobody won.

他們的舉動只會打壞市場，誰都賺不到錢。

⑦ availability：可使用性、可用性

Regarding the dispatching date, it depends on the availability of the product.

關於出貨日期，那得看是否有現貨而定。

⑧ are you free to talk now?：現在方便說話嗎？

⑨ how's it going?：你好嗎？

這是對平輩，而且有一定交情的對象較適用的句子，否則還是得用較符合傳統禮節的 how are you? 或是 how are you doing?

⑩ I'd like to…：我想要…

這是最基本的口語用詞，避免使用過多的 want，因為 want 的詞意較直接、強勢

I'd like to remind you of the overdue payment of $36,000.

我想提醒你一筆 36000 美金的逾期款項。

⑪ is it OK with you?：（某件事）你方便嗎？

介系詞用 with，不要用 for

⑫ hold on a second：（請）等一下

也可說 wait a second 或 just a second

Hold on a second. Are you saying that we won't get the goods until next week?

等一下，你是說我們要等到下星期才能收到貨嗎？

文重點② Summary 2

In today's super-busy business world, reaching customers over the phone isn't an easy task, let alone making an appointment to meet them face to face. Very often, salespeople have to try again and again to work out a visit plan with the customers. The worst-case scenario, namely last-minute cancellation, happens from time to time.

這是業務經常會碰上的情形，要順利約到對方並不容易，往往得邀約好幾次才成功。最怕的是那種臨時變卦，人都已到現場卻因故無法相見的情形。

預約洽商 2　Making An Appointment 2 1-2

> **Steve**：**Account Manager, Adventure Computer** 客戶經理
>
> **Cindy**：**PM, MIB Electronics** 專案經理

Steve：Hi Cindy, this is Steve Weeks from Adventure Computer. Are you free to talk now?

嗨 Cindy，我是 Adventure Computer 的 Steve Weeks，現在方便說話嗎？

Cindy：Sorry Steve, I am busy now. I'll call you back later.

抱歉，Steve，我在忙，等會兒回你電話。

Steve：OK, thanks.

多謝啦！

(later...)

Cindy：Hi Steve, this is Cindy Pride of MIB Electronics. You were looking for me?

嗨 Steve，我是 MIB 公司的 Cindy Pride。你剛剛找我嗎？

Steve：Yes, it's about Project Sun. I'd like to discuss with you. Is Wednesday morning or Thursday afternoon OK with you?

對呀！是有關 Sun 的案子，我想和妳討論一下。
妳星期三上午或星期四下午方便嗎？

Cindy：I'm sorry. I'll be very busy this week. Can you call me next Monday?

很抱歉，我這個星期都很忙，你能下週一再打給我嗎？

☺ Steve ： I see. OK, I'll call you on Monday. <u>Have a nice day!</u>
了解。那我下星期一再打電話給妳。祝妳愉快！

☺ Cindy ： Thank you. <u>Talk to you later.</u>
謝謝，再聊。

NOTE

❶ super-busy：非常忙碌的、超忙的

Sorry Ken, I can't help you with your technical report. I'll be super-busy this week.

抱歉 Ken，那份技術報告我沒法幫你什麼忙，我這星期超忙的。

❷ reach：到達、伸出

這裡是指「接觸到」的意思

How to reach the right customer base becomes a real challenge to a marketing person.

如何接觸到正確的客戶群成了行銷人員的一大挑戰。

❸ over the phone：以電話（聯繫、討論）

Why don't we discuss it over the phone first?

我們為何不先用電話討論呢？

至於也很常說的 on the phone 則是指「在打電話」的意思

Sorry, Dan is on the phone now. May I take the message?

對不起，Dan 現在電話中，您要留話嗎？

NOTE

④ **task**：任務、工作

⑤ **let alone**：更不用說、遑論

Poor customer service will put us in a shaky position, let alone poor product quality.

差勁的客服會讓我們陷入危局，更別說是差勁的產品品質了。

⑥ **face to face**：面對面

I suggest that you visit them right away and discuss the issue face to face.

我建議你馬上就去拜訪他們，當面討論這議題。

⑦ **very often**：經常

Very often, Richard and I exchange market information to update each other.

Richard 和我經常交換最新的市場訊息。

⑧ **work out**：做出、規劃出

Don't worry, Jane. We will soon work out a solution to solve the problem.

別擔心 Jane，我們很快就會找到解決問題的辦法。

⑨ **the worst-case scenario**：最糟糕的狀況

Take it easy, Tom. The worst-case scenario is that we lose the order.

放輕鬆些，Tom。最壞的情況就只是丟單而已。

NOTE

⑩ last-minute cancellation：最後臨時取消

Vincent, you'd better make sure this time. The last-minute cancellation you made last week almost ruined my entire weekly work plan.

Vincent，這次你最好要確定啊！上星期你最後臨時取消訂單，差點沒毀了我一整週的工作計畫。

⑪ from time to time：不時、時常

From time to time, salespeople feel tired while moving from one country to the other.

業務人員在不同國家間往來時，常常會覺得疲倦。

⑫ call you back：回電

不要用 call back you

⑬ you were looking for me?：「你剛才找我？」的口語說法

⑭ It's about：是關於

My boss just sent me a reminder. It's about the blanket order to which you committed last week.

我老闆剛剛發了一則提醒簡訊給我，是有關於上星期你承諾的長期預估訂單。

⑮ have a nice day!：祝你愉快！

也是「再見」的意思

NOTE

⑯ **talk to you later.**：再聊。

Lisa, I have to go now. Talk to you later.

Lisa，我得走了，再聊囉！

重點③ **Summary 3**

Much more attention should be paid to overseas business trips in order to make them more productive. Be it budgeted or ad-hoc, everything from objective setting, scheduling, to meeting agenda preparing, repetitive checking and confirming with the clients would be necessary. It is particularly true for the first-time visits as the salesperson is usually alone and without too much internal or external support.

業務人員拜訪國外客戶，為了確保拜訪成效與效率，需要注意的就更多了。無論是定期或是突發性拜訪，從出訪目的規劃、拜訪行程確認，討論事項準備等細節，都必須在出訪前再三與客戶確認。尤其初次拜訪客戶，因為多半得獨自前往，無論自行開車或搭車，都要先查問清楚，以免臨時出狀況，延誤拜訪時間。

預約洽商3　Making An Appointment 3 1-3

Steve ： **Sales Rep, Adventure Computer** 業務代表

Nicole ： **Purchaser, MIB Electronics** 採購

Steve： Hi Nicole, this is Steve Weeks from Adventure Computer. How are you doing today?

嗨 Nicole，我是 Adventure Computer 的 Steve Weeks，妳今天好嗎？

Nicole： Hi Steve, I'm just fine, thank you. I received your e-mail regarding your visiting plans next month. Yes, it's better we meet again.

嗨 Steve，我很好啊！謝謝。我收到你發的下個月來拜訪那封信了。沒錯，我們最好再碰個面了。

Steve： Awesome! Would you please check the plan and <u>confirm acceptance</u> ASAP?

太好了！能麻煩妳看一下我的拜訪計畫，並確認可行嗎？

Dr. Lee 解析

國外業務出訪，大多會拜訪同區域內多國、多家客戶。安排完整行程費時費工，因為客戶時程也會不時變動。所以業務應適時提醒每家客戶，早些確認拜訪行程。

Nicole：I did. And I also talked with those who were on your meeting list. I'll get back to you later today.

我看過了，也通知了名單上的同事，今天稍晚我會回覆你。

Dr. Lee 解析

每次會議討論的議題確定時，也要儘早通知與會相關人員，屆時參加會議。

Steve：Thanks. I need your <u>feedback</u> to <u>finalize my trip plan</u> sooner.

謝謝。我得早些收到妳的回覆，以便敲定最後行程。

(later...)

Nicole：Hello Steve, this is Nicole. I'd like to tell you that a meeting with you in the morning of May 21 has been <u>scheduled</u> as you requested.

哈囉 Steve，我是 Nicole。我已經根據你的要求，安排在 5 月 21 號上午一起開會。

Dr. Lee 解析

遠行出訪能圓滿達成既定目標很重要，客戶端的配合與協助是關鍵。

Steve：Thanks for your quick response. How about the <u>proposed meeting agenda</u> I worked out for the meeting? Do you like to add any more <u>topics</u>?

感謝妳這麼快就回覆。妳們覺得我提出的討論議題如何？要增加任何討論事項嗎？

Dr. Lee 解析

> 決定好會議主要討論事項是必須的，好讓雙方都能事先準備，確保效率。

Nicole : No, you've covered all the <u>issues</u> we have <u>on hand</u>. We'll let you know if there's anything new <u>worth</u> discussing.

沒有，所有該討論的你都放上去了。若還有想到，會通知你的。

Steve : That's great. Will you be able to <u>pick me up from the train station</u> as you did last time? It wasn't very easy to find a <u>cab</u> there during <u>rush hour</u>.

那太好了。這次還能請妳和上次一樣，到火車站來接我嗎？上下班尖峰時段，車站那兒很難等到計程車。

Dr. Lee 解析

> 出差國外，若能得到客戶各方面的協助最理想，業務最好隨身準備好適當禮物致謝。

Nicole : <u>Not a problem.</u> Just let me know the <u>ETA</u> and I'll be there <u>in time</u>.

沒問題。告訴我預定到達時間，我會及時趕到的。

Dr. Lee 解析

別忘了將確切的 ETA 告訴對方。

Steve : Thanks so much. I'll send you everything <u>concerning</u> the meeting by e-mail <u>once it becomes available</u>.

真是謝謝妳。一旦我準備好開會的所有相關資料，會馬上用電郵傳給妳。

Dr. Lee 解析

務必記得將所有交談內容的細節，以 e-mail 方式傳給對方，作為共同遵循依據。

Nicole : Cool. And welcome to MIB again.

好的，歡迎你再次光臨囉！

NOTE

❶ attention should be paid to：注意、留意於某方面

常見的是主動式的 pay attention to。這裡改用被動式，實際上同義

Special attention should be paid to the technical specifications while we're handling a system project.

當我們在處理一個系統專案時，應該特別注意技術規格。

❷ overseas business trip：國外商務出差

❸ in order to：為了、以便

Many salespeople choose to sleep during flight in order to get more rest.

許多業務人員選擇在飛行途中睡覺以便能多休息。

❹ productive：有生產力的

In order to stay competitive in the industry, each and every one in the company has to become more productive.

為了能在產業中保持競爭力，公司上下每位員工得變得更有生產力。

❺ budgeted：在預算內的

A total of 7 overseas business trips have been budgeted in our annual sales plan.

在我們年度業務預算中一共編列了 7 趟國外出差。

6 ad hoc：臨時的、特別的

Because of the recent quality issue, an ad hoc trip to Japan Steel by our CTO has been scheduled.

由於最近的品管事件，我們的 CTO（技術長）臨時安排了一趟至 Japan Steel 的行程。

7 objective setting：目標設定

8 scheduling：行程排定

9 meeting agenda：開會議程

10 repetitive：重複的

Repetitive mistakes like this are totally unacceptable.

我完全無法接受像這樣重複犯錯。

11 confirm with：與…確認

Terry, after confirming with our main supplier, I'm sorry to tell you that we won't be getting any incoming materials for the night shift.

Terry，在和我們主要供應商確認之後，抱歉我得告訴你，原料將趕不上今天夜班作業。

12 necessary：必需的、必要的

It is absolutely necessary to sum up the discussions and the conclusions at the end of the meeting.

在會議結束時，總結所有討論與結論是絕對有必要的。

NOTE

⑬ particularly：尤其、特別的

So far our sales performance has been quite impressive, particularly in the past April.

至今我們的業績表現相當不錯，尤其是四月份。

⑭ internal：內部的

⑮ external：外部的

⑯ confirm acceptance：確認能否接受

I have already sent you the preliminary itinerary of my visit to your factory next week. Would you please check and confirm acceptance?

我已將下星期要去拜訪你們工廠的初步行程傳給你了，請你核對並且確認能否接受好嗎？

⑰ feedback：回饋、回覆

Please send your feedback to me once you finish reading the market report.

一旦看完這份市場報告，請將你的意見回覆給我。

⑱ finalize my trip plan：完成出差計畫

⑲ schedule：排定

The meeting has been scheduled on Wednesday morning.

會議被安排在週三上午。

NOTE

⑳ propose：提出

How about the proposed itinerary? Do you like it?

我所提出的行程如何？你們喜歡嗎？

㉑ meeting agenda：會議議程

㉒ topic：話題、主題

㉓ issue：未決議題

I realize there are a number of issues regarding manufacturing bottleneck.

我了解在製造瓶頸上有許多沒解決的問題。

㉔ on hand：在手上、在手中

How many do you need? I've got plenty of them on hand.

你需要多少？我手邊還有很多。

㉕ worth：值得，後接動名詞

I think the issue is worth discussing once again.

我認為這議題值得再討論一次。

㉖ pick me up from the train station：來火車站接我，介系詞用**from**而不用**at**

㉗ cab：計程車，也可說**taxi**

I think we'd better take a cab to save some time.

我認為我們最好搭小黃以便節省一點時間。

NOTE

㉘ **rush hour**：交通尖峰時間

㉙ **not a problem**：不成問題、沒問題，同**no problem**

㉚ **ETA**：預計到達時間，**Estimated Time of Arrival** 的縮寫

㉛ **in time**：及時

The shipment arrived at our warehouse in time for production.

那批貨及時送達我們倉庫趕上生產。

㉜ **concerning**：關於

Concerning the coming factory auditing by Appleton, Jack has been assigned as the executive coordinator of the task force.

關於即將到來的 Appleton 工廠稽核，Jack 已被選派為任務編組總協調。

㉝ **once it becomes available**：一旦準備好、處理好

The photo? I will call you once it becomes available.

相片嗎？一旦處理完成，我會打電話給你。

Lesson ② 客戶要求報價
Request for Quotation(RFQ)

課文重點① **Summary 1**

Handling RFQ is one of the routines that salespeople need to do almost every day. Very often it is so tedious and time-consuming that sometimes salespeople would feel very tired. Yet the RFQ is so important that any mistake could cause serious damage to the company. Thanks to the internet and all the mobile devices, the timing of responding to customer's RFQ becomes a lot more critical. Nowadays, most customers have requested that suppliers respond to their RFQs within 24 hours.

處理 RFQ 是業務幾乎天天都得做的工作，由於報價單內容層次很多，處理費時並需要很高的專注力，容易讓業務人員覺得倦怠，因而將報價工作轉給業助處理。然而業務必須體認，若因 RFQ 沒處理好而出錯，將會給公司帶來大災難。此外，由於行動通訊快速發展，業務人員藉由個人行動裝置，及時處理客戶緊急要求的機率大增，客戶往往要求供應商在24小時內書面回覆 RFQ。

單純的 RFQ Simple RFQ  2-1

> **Sam** ：**Purchaser, Adventure Computer (Singapore)** 採購
>
> **Christine** ：**Sales Rep, Umax Inc. (Taiwan)** 業務代表

Sam：Hi Christine, this is Sam Martin, purchaser of Adventure Computer. How are you doing?

嗨 Christine，我是 Adventure Computer 的採購 Sam Martin。妳好嗎？

Christine：Just fine, Sam, thanks. How may I help you?

謝謝你，Sam，我很好。有什麼我能替你服務的嗎？

Sam：I'm trying to find an ultrasonic cleaning machine of good quality.

我正在找高品質的超音波清洗機。

Christine：Good, which model are you referring to?

好啊，你是指哪個型號的？

Sam：I saw it on your web site. The model name is AD-7.

我從妳們網站上看到的型號是 AD-7。

Christine：Oh, it is one of our new models. What is the application?

噢，那是我們的一臺新機種。你們要應用在哪裡？

Sam：Grease removal.

去除油脂。

Christine: Then AD-7 should be a perfect fit. Have you checked the specs yet?

那麼 AD-7 最適合了，規格你核對過了嗎？

Sam: Yes, I did. We need the 120 k Hertz type, 220VAC power. What's your selling price?

核對過了，我們要的是 120 千赫，220 交流電。這臺售價多少？

Christine: How many units will you buy this time?

你們這次想要買幾臺？

Sam: Only three. Is there any discount for three units?

只要 3 臺，一次買 3 臺會有折扣嗎？

Christine: I'm afraid not, very sorry.

抱歉，沒有。

Sam: I see. When will you send me your quotation?

這樣啊！那妳什麼時候能傳報價單給我？

Christine: In about 30 minutes. Should I send it to your e-mail or fax machine?

半小時吧！要傳到你的 e-mail 還是傳真機？

Sam: Please send to my e-mail box as soon as possible, thanks.

請儘快傳到我的 e-mail。謝啦！

Christine: No problem, thanks very much.

沒問題，謝謝。

Sam: Thank you. Bye.

多謝，再見了。

NOTE

❶ handling：處理

Handling a customer complaint isn't as easy as you might think.

處理客戶的抱怨並非如你想的那麼容易。

❷ RFQ：請求、要求報價

產業界中還有另一種較複雜的 request for proposal 請求提案，簡稱 RFP

❸ routine：例行公事、常規性工作

Marketing or sales, you just can't get away with the routines.

無論是行銷或業務，你都無法避免例行公事。

❹ very often：經常、時常

Very often, we're forced to compete by undercutting competitors under the pressure of short-term sales target.

由於受到短期業績壓力影響，我們常常被迫得低報價格搶訂單。

❺ tedious：單調乏味的、沉悶的

Processing an RFQ can be extremely tedious and tiresome.

處理報價請求是一件極端單調乏味而且累人的事。

❻ time-consuming：費時的、耗時的

Cold calling can be very time-consuming and ineffective.

冷拜訪（不熟識拜訪）耗時效果又不佳。

Cold calling 多半是指利用電話與完全陌生或沒預期、沒意願和你對談的對象進行業務拜訪

⑦ **damage**：損害、傷害

⑧ **thanks to**：由於、多虧

Recently, thanks to the internet and social media, a lot of reunions have been made possible.

近年來，多虧了網際網路與社群媒體，促成了許多重聚和團圓的佳話。

⑨ **mobile device**：行動裝置

Smartphones, tablets, and wearables are the major types of mobile devices.

智慧型手機、平板電腦和可穿戴裝置是最主要的行動裝置種類。

⑩ **respond to**：回應、回覆

I have been busy responding to more than 20 RFQs ever since I sat down to work earlier this morning.

自從我今早坐下開始工作以後，我一直在忙著回覆超過 20 件報價請求。

⑪ **a lot more**：多很多、非常多，也可說 **much more**

I traveled a lot more this year than I did last year.

今年我出差要比去年頻繁得多。

⑫ **critical**：緊要的、關鍵的

Customer service is too critical to ignore.

客服實在太關鍵，絕不可忽視。

NOTE

⑬ **request**：要求、請求

Randy requested that each salesperson visit at least 10 customers in a week.

Randy 要求每位業務人員每週至少拜訪 10 家客戶。

⑭ **how may I help you?**：我能幫你什麼忙嗎？請問有何貴幹？

一種很有禮貌的說法

⑮ **ultrasonic cleaning machine**：超音波清洗機

⑯ **which model are you referring to?**：你是指哪個機型？

這裡的 referring to 是指「哪一個」機種型號

I'm sorry sir. What order number were you referring to?

先生，對不起，你剛剛是指哪個訂單號碼？

⑰ **application**：應用或應用場合

工業產品多以用途來做市場區隔，並針對不同用途開發適用產品

Our main application is paint mixing in hazardous area.

我們主要應用是在危險區域內做油漆混和攪拌。

⑱ **grease removal**：去除油脂

⑲ **specs**：規格，**specifications**的縮寫

NOTE

⑳ **discount**：折扣

Usually, the channel partner discount ranges from 20% to 50%, depending on the customer class.

一般來說，通路夥伴折扣會在 20% 與 50% 之間，視客戶等級而定。

㉑ **I'm afraid not.**：恐怕沒有、很遺憾沒有

㉒ **quotation**：報價單

課文重點② **Summary 2**

Usually, in addition to a price quote and the quantity of the specified items, an RFQ would also include many other transaction terms such as payment terms (method, duration, etc.), delivery terms (place, schedule, penalty, etc.), and services (VMI, warranty, etc.). Therefore, it is indeed very important for a salesperson to pay close attention to RFQ processing. Otherwise, if something goes wrong and the customer fails to receive what they expected, the damages to the company could be enormous.

一般來說，在 RFQ 內容裡，客戶除了列出詢價標的物名稱、規格與數量外，還會清楚列出其他交易相關條件，如付款條件（方式、期限等）、交貨條件（地點、批次、罰則等）以及服務項目（中繼倉、保固等）。這些都是交易的重要條件，業務人員在進行報價之前，必須仔細審閱各項條件。倘若因疏忽而導致交易不成，或履行訂單發生糾紛，都會造成公司鉅額損失，不可不慎。

 複雜的 RFQ　More Complicated RFQ 2-2

> **Sam**：**Purchaser, Adventure Computer (Singapore)** 採購
>
> **Christine**：**Sales Rep., Umax Inc. (Taiwan)** 業務代表

Sam：Hi Christine , this is Sam Martin from Adventure Computer. How are you doing today?

嗨 Christine，我是 Adventure 電腦公司的 Sam Martin，妳今天好嗎？

Christine：Hi Sam, pretty good, thank you. How about yourself?

嗨！Sam，我很好啊！謝謝。你呢？

Dr. Lee 解析

在這裡，我們當然可以用最常聽到的「And you?」代替「How about yourself？」

Sam：Very busy. I just sent a new RFQ to you via e-mail. Did you see it?

我非常忙碌。剛才我用 e-mail 傳了一份新的 RFQ 給妳，看到了嗎？

Christine：You did? OK, I'll check right away. Oh, I've got it. Hmm, a complicated one, isn't it?

你傳了啊？好，我馬上查查看。噢！我收到了。嗯…還挺複雜的對吧？

Dr. Lee 解析

這裡的「You did?」是很常用的口語問句用法，語調必須在 did 一字時拉高。句尾的「isn't it?」反問句是在反問 Hmm, a complicated one.

Sam : Well, not too bad. But I guess I'd better explain to you over the phone first.

還好啦！不過我最好先在電話裡向妳解釋一下。

Dr. Lee 解析

在這句中，「I guess ...」也能說成「I think ...」。

Christine : Yes, please do. I'm not quite sure I'll be able to comprehend all these terms, particularly the specs of those items. It's Greek to me as I can hardly recognize any of them.

是的，麻煩請你解釋一下。我沒把握能完全理解這些專業用語，尤其是產品規格。我看不懂，幾乎完全不認識這些規格。

Dr. Lee 解析

處理 RFQ，必須細心看清楚細節，耐心讀懂條文。

Sam : OK , I'll be glad to explain to you now. Actually the items you saw <u>belong to</u> one of your competitors, namely Dewalt Precisions.

好的，我很樂意解釋給妳聽。實際上，妳看到的項目是屬於妳們競爭對手之一，Dewalt Precisions 的產品編號。

Dr. Lee 解析

這裡採購用參考設計（refernece design）方式要求廠商報價。

Christine : <u>I got your point</u>. Yeah, Dewalt has been <u>competing head-on with</u> us in some applications. So I guess you want us to quote for our <u>compatibles</u>?

我懂了。沒錯，Dewalt 一直在某些應用上和我們競爭得很厲害。所以我猜你是要我提供公司相容產品的價格。

Dr. Lee 解析

根據同行競爭者的產品特性規格，選擇自家相容產品報價。

Sam : <u>Exactly</u>. I'll be sending all the technical specs and other <u>relevant</u> information regarding these items to you soon.

正是如此。我會儘快把技術規格和其他產品相關資料傳給妳。

Dr. Lee 解析

切記買賣雙方任何對話內容，必須以書面格式做最後確認，成為雙方責任義務的遵循準則。

Christine : Thanks very much. I do need that information to proceed.
多謝了。我確實需要那些資訊以便開始作業。

Dr. Lee 解析

處理 RFQ 如此重要的交易文件，每項步驟都要有憑有據。

Sam : There are some more issues I'd like to remind you to pay special attention to.
還有些事項我想要提醒妳特別留意。

Dr. Lee 解析

除了提供價格數據，RFQ 裡還有其他重要事項需特別注意。

Christine : OK. What are the issues?
好的，是哪些呢？

Sam : The most important one is that we changed the trade term from FCA to DDP. The revision is so significant that our suppliers may have to re-calculate the total cost of supplying to us.

最重要的一點是，我們把貿易條件由 FCA 改成 DDP。這是很重大的改變，將導致供應廠商必須重新計算供應成本。

Dr. Lee 解析

RFQ 裡，貿易條件直接影響到買賣雙方所承擔的風險以及交易成本。由 FCA 變成 DDP，可說是非常極端修正的例子。

Christine : From FCA, Free Carrier, to DDP, Delivered Duty Paid? It is indeed a big change. The differences include the freight, duty, and all the handling fees up to the specified delivery place.

由 FCA「貨交運送公司條件」變為 DDP「稅訖交貨條件」？那絕對是一項大改變。其中的差異包括運費、關稅以及由裝貨地至交貨指定地之間的一切處理費用。

Dr. Lee 解析

買賣雙方的詳細權利義務，業務必須仔細檢視、詳細核對。

Sam : In addition, please pay attention to the product warranty of this RFQ as we need a longer warranty period of 18 months, 6 months longer than the normal one.

除此之外，請注意這份 RFQ 裡，我們要求 18 個月的產品保固期，比一般的 12 個月多了 6 個月。

Dr. Lee 解析

RFQ 裡各項重要交易條件，可能會隨著客戶本身需求而改變。報價廠商必須逐次逐項檢查，避免因疏忽而出錯。這裡是有關保固期的更改。

Christine : OK, I'll discuss with our Q.A. manager regarding this.

好，我會和我們的品保經理討論這點。

Sam : Anyway, please read the RFQ carefully to avoid any miscue while processing it.

無論如何，請仔細檢視這份 RFQ，避免在處理過程中發生錯誤。

Christine : I surely will, Sam. Thanks very much.

我一定會的。Sam，非常謝謝你。

NOTE

❶ transaction：交易

Our ERP system is so powerful that it tracks and analyzes every single transaction of the responsible salesperson almost on a real time basis.

我們的 ERP 系統功能非常強，它能以幾近即時的方式追蹤並分析每位業務人員的每筆交易。

❷ duration：期間

The trade show lasts for 4 days. I will have to stay here for the entire duration.

這貿易展將持續 4 天，這段期間我都得待在這裡。

NOTE

❸ penalty：懲罰、罰款、罰則

Salespeople must be very careful dealing with the penalty clause on the purchase order.

業務人員對於訂單上的懲罰條款必須非常小心處理。

❹ VMI：原物料供應商提供並管理之近距庫存

VMI 為 Vendor Managed Inventory 的縮寫

Providing EMS customers with VMI service has become essential for a supplier to gain a chance as a second source.

供應商提供 EMS 客戶 VMI 服務，已成為一個爭取變成替代供應商資格的必要條件。

❺ warranty：保證、保固

Our standard product warranty is 18 months.

我們標準產品的保固期是 18 個月。

❻ pay close attention：密切注意

As peak season is approaching, we need to pay close attention to both capacity planning and materials procurement.

隨著旺季到來，我們得密切注意產能規劃和物料採購。

❼ otherwise：否則、不然

Listen carefully to what your customers say. Otherwise, you're not going to win their trust.

你得仔細聆聽客戶的說法，否則你將無法贏得他們的信任。

NOTE

⑧ go wrong：出錯、出問題

Don't panic if something goes wrong.

如果出了問題，先別慌張。

⑨ fail to：沒能、無法

Philip fails to convince the customer to place order.

Philip 沒能說服客戶下單。

⑩ enormous：巨大的、極大的

The company invested an enormous amount of money in expanding its manufacturing capacity.

那家公司注入了龐大資金來擴大產能。

⑪ you did?：是嗎？

指 Sam 上句話所說的：「剛才我用 e-mail 傳了一份新 RFQ 給你」那件事

John: "Sandy, I put the book on your doorstep. Did you see it?" Sandy: "You did? I'll go get it now."

John：「Sandy，我把書放在妳門階上了，看到了嗎？」
Sandy：「是嗎？我馬上就去拿。」

⑫ right away：立刻、馬上

也可說 right now 或 immediately

Don't worry, Jane. I'll correct it right away.

別擔心，Jane。我立刻就改過來。

⑬ **I've got it**：我看到了、我找到了

⑭ **complicated**：複雜的，也可說**complex**

I'm asking our FAE to help me with this complicated application problem.

我正要求我們的應用工程師協助解決這複雜的應用問題。

⑮ **I'd better**：我最好是…

I had better 的縮寫，後面的動詞要用原形

It's raining. I'd better put on my rain jacket.

下雨了，我最好穿上雨衣。

⑯ **over the phone**：在電話交談中

Frank, don't worry. I've told your wife over the phone earlier today.

Frank，別擔心。今天稍早我已經在電話中告訴你太太了。

⑰ **I'm not quite sure**：我不是很確定

也可說 I'm not too sure 或 I'm not so sure.

I'm not quite sure if I should tell Wendy about the possible delay of the cargo flight.

我不知是否該告訴 Wendy 貨機可能會延後抵達。

NOTE

⑱ comprehend：理解、了解，也可說**understand**

To a new guy like Alex, the technical part of the training might be a bit too hard to comprehend.

訓練課程中的技術部分，對 Alex 這樣的新人來說，或許會有點難理解。

⑲ it's Greek to me：我看不懂

The operations manual is so difficult to read. It's Greek to me!

這操作手冊好難理解，我真的看不懂。

⑳ can hardly：幾乎無法

hardly 若用在句子開頭時，要用倒裝句型：Hardly can I recognize any of them. 可改爲 I can hardly recognize any of them.

Hardly can I believe what I just saw.

我幾乎無法相信剛才我所看到的。

㉑ recognize：辨識、認出

Kevin failed to recognize the exact cartons that he intended to take delivery among so many similar others from the customs.

Kevin 沒法在那麼多外觀相似的貨箱中，確切地辨識出他打算清關提貨的那幾箱貨。

㉒ belong to：屬於

The laptop on the receptionist's desk belongs to David.

在接待桌上的那臺筆電是屬於 David 的。

NOTE

㉓ **I got your point.** : 我了解你的意思、我了解你所說的

㉔ **compete head-on with** : 正面激烈競爭

head-on 也可以用 head-to- head 代替

We have been competing head-to-head with Dell for more than 10 years.

我們和戴爾電腦正面激烈交鋒已經超過 10 年。

㉕ **compatible** : 相容品

It's easy to find as many compatibles as you'd like from the market.

相容產品在市面上很容易就能找到，想要多少就有多少。

㉖ **exactly** : 正是如此、一點沒錯、完全正確

Exactly David, we will hit the sales target as we budgeted.

一點沒錯，David，我們會如預算那樣達成銷售目標。

㉗ **relevant** : 相關的、適當的

You need to supply us with more relevant technical information.

你得提供更多的技術資訊給我們。

㉘ **do need** : 的確需要

助動詞 do、does、did 放在主動詞前乃為加強語氣用法

We do need your immediate support.

我們的確需要你們立即提供支援。

NOTE

㉙ **proceed**：繼續、著手去做

Please make up your mind now so that we can proceed.

請你現在就做決定，好讓我們能著手進行。

㉚ **pay special attention to**：特別注意在…上
在此別把 to 給漏說了

Helen, don't forget those reminders that you must pay special attention to.

Helen，別忘了那些得特別留意的提醒事項。

㉛ **trade terms**：貿易條件

Many new trade terms have been included in ICC Incoterms 2010 version.

在 2010 年新國貿條規裡包含了好多新的貿易條件。

㉜ **FCA (ICC Incoterms 2010：2010年新國貿條規)**：貨交運送公司條件
Free Carrier 的縮寫

㉝ **DDP (ICC Incoterms 2010：2010年新國貿條規)**：稅訖交貨條件
Delivered Duty Paid 的縮寫

NOTE

㉞ revision：修正、修訂

Please send us the revisions as early as possible since keeping our database updated is crucial to us.

請儘早將修正內容傳給我們，因為隨時更新資料庫對我們非常重要。

㉟ significant：重要的、重大的

The significant change in buyer behavior has forced our salespeople to work smarter.

採購行為的重大改變，迫使我們的業務人員得多用頭腦工作。

㊱ re-calculate：重新計算

The ever-increasing price of stainless steel forced us to re-calculate our manufacturing cost.

不鏽鋼價格不斷飆漲，迫使我們得重新計算製造成本。

㊲ indeed：真的、確實

A friend in need is a friend indeed.

患難見真情。

Punctual delivery is indeed important to us.

準時交貨對我們真的很重要。

㊳ duty：稅金

We pay an enormous amount of duty to the customs every year.

我們每年付給海關金額很高的關稅。

NOTE

㊵ handling fee：處理費用、手續費

I don't know why we have to pay the banks so much handling fees.

我不明白我們為什麼得付這麼多手續費給銀行。

㊵ specified delivery place：特別指定的交貨地點

㊶ in addition：此外、另外

也可說 additionally 或 besides

In addition, we need to improve our profitability.

此外，我們還得改善獲利率。

㊷ product warranty：產品保固

Product warranty is an important part of our quality assurance system.

產品保固是品保系統中的一個重要部分。

㊸ Q.A.：品保、品質保證

Quality Assurance 的縮寫

㊹ anyway：無論如何、總之

Like it or not, we salespeople will have to step up and resolve the tough problems anyway.

無論喜歡與否，我們做業務的終究還是得扛起責任解決難題。

45 miscue：錯誤、失誤

多用於口語，也可說 mistake 或 error

Too many miscues in our customer service cost us a good customer.

我們客服過多的錯誤讓我們丟掉了一個好客戶。

Lesson ③ Price Negotiation 議價

文重點① Summary 1

Negotiating prices is <u>probably</u> the most <u>common</u> daily <u>interaction</u> between sellers and buyers as pricing is one of the most important <u>variables</u> in almost every business <u>transaction</u>. For most <u>industrial products</u>, <u>components</u> or <u>equipment</u>, selling prices may <u>vary</u> with the quantity purchased.

議價是買賣雙方談生意時最常見的互動行為。買方採購往往在收到賣方報價單後，向賣方業務提出降價需求。多數工業產品，無論屬零組件或設備，賣方多願意按買方購買數量來決定議價空間。

議價 1　Price Negotiation 1　 3-1

Sam：**Purchaser, Adventure Computer (Singapore)** 採購

Christine：**Sales Rep, Umax Inc. (Taiwan)** 業務代表

Sam：Hi Christine, this is Sam Martin, purchaser of Adventure Computer. How are you doing?

嗨 Christine，我是 Adventure Computer 的採購 Sam Martin。妳好嗎？

Christine：Just fine, thanks. Did you receive the quotation I sent to you yesterday?

謝謝你，我很好。你有收到我昨天傳給你的報價單嗎？

Sam：Yes, I did. In fact I'm calling to discuss with you about the price.

收到了，我打這通電話就是要和妳討論報價的。

Christine：Oh yeah? You don't like it?

是嗎？你不滿意嗎？

Sam：No, I don't because it's <u>too high</u>, <u>much too high</u>, <u>to</u> accept.

是的。價格太高了，我們無法接受。

Christine：Trust me please. It is <u>the lowest</u> we can offer for a small order of ten units.

請相信我，你們只買 10 臺，這已經是最低價了。

Sam：Please do me a favor and consider a 10% reduction.
請幫個忙，看看能不能降 10%。

Christine：I'm very sorry, it's the lowest we can go. But if you can increase the quantity to twenty units, I can further talk with my boss.
真的抱歉，我無法再降了。如果你們能一次買 20 臺，我來和主管爭取看看。

Sam：What? You said 20 units? And we'll get 10% discount?
什麼？你說 20 臺？然後我們可以有 10% 折扣？

Christine：Yes, 10% discount for a 20-unit purchasing order.
是的，給 10% 折扣，換你們一張 20 臺的訂單。

Sam：OK, I'll check with our end customer and call you back soon. Thanks.
好，我去和客戶討論一下，等會兒回妳電話，謝謝。

Christine：No problem. Talk to you later.
沒問題，待會兒聊。

NOTE

① **probably**：可能、或許、大概
You probably don't know how much the market price of stainless steel has increased in recent months.
你大概不了解近幾個月來不鏽鋼市場價格上漲了多少。

② **common**：常見的、普遍的
Price competition is one of the most common modes of competition.
價格競爭是幾種常見競爭模式之一。

NOTE

❸ interaction：互動、相互作用

In a B2B model, the quality of buyer-seller relationships depends mainly on the interactions between the two.

在 B2B 模式裡，買賣雙方關係的品質，主要視雙方互動密切與否而定。

❹ variable：變數

Before we start to calculate the pricing scheme for different customer group, we need to decide what variables we should take into account.

在開始替不同客戶群計算定價方案前，我們得決定需要考慮那些變數。

❺ transaction：交易

To upgrade our customer service quality, each of us has to pay close attention to every single transaction in the process.

要提升我們的客服品質，我們每個人都要多留意流程中的每一宗交易。

❻ industrial product：工業產品

The sales strategy of industrial products differs from that of consumer products.

工業產品的銷售策略與消費產品的銷售策略不同。

NOTE

7 component：零組件

Selling components is different from selling a complete system in terms of technical complexity.

以技術複雜度來說，賣零組件和賣成套系統是不一樣的。

8 equipment：設備

When buying a whole set of equipment, the customer would request that the supplier provide a complete turnkey solution.

每當客戶採購一整套設備時，都會要求供應廠商提供統包解決方案。

9 vary：變動、變異、改變

Market price of many key components may vary every week, even every day.

許多關鍵零組件的市場價格每週，甚至每天，都在變動。

10 oh yeah?：是嗎？

有 Is it what you think? 的意思，口說英語常用

Oh yeah? How did they quote anyway?

是嗎？到底他們如何報價的？

11 too + 形 + to + 動：太⋯而無法⋯

I'm sorry, Jason. The price you quoted this morning is too high to accept.

抱歉 Jason，你早上報的價格太高，我們無法接受。

NOTE

⑫ **much too high**：高太多、太高

The carton was too heavy, much too heavy, to move without a warehouse cart.

這箱子實在太重。若沒有一臺倉庫用推車,是沒法搬動的。

⑬ **the lowest**：最低的

Frank, this is the lowest price we can offer. I can't go any lower.

Frank,這是我們能給的最低報價,沒法再低了。

⑭ **do me a favor**：幫（我）個忙

Would you please do me a favor by telling me which platform to take for the 11:30 train to London?

能請你幫我個忙,告訴我 11:30 往倫敦的火車,該從哪個月臺上車?

⑮ **consider**：考慮

Would you please consider the price I suggested yesterday morning?

請你考慮一下昨天早上我建議的價格好嗎?

⑯ **reduction**：降低、減少

Any reduction in our MSP will place us in a poor financial position.

倘若還要降低我們的 MSP,那會使我們陷入財務困境。

MSP 是 Minimum Selling Price（最低售價）的縮寫

NOTE

⑰ **it is the lowest we can go**：我們最低只能降到這個程度

⑱ **further**：進一步地

If you agree on this price, I'll go back and further convince my boss to increase your allocation from 25% to 50%.

如果你們同意給這價格，我回去就再進一步說服我老闆，將你們的配額從 25% 增加到 50%。

⑲ **check with**：詢問、核對

If you locked yourself out of your hotel room, please go and check with the front desk for help.

如果你把自己鎖在旅館房間外，請直接去服務櫃檯請求協助。

⑳ **end customer**：終端客戶，指代理商或經銷商的客戶

We don't sell direct to end customers. We sell through dealers.

我們不直接賣給終端客戶，我們透過經銷商販賣。

㉑ **talk to you later.** 稍後再談、待會聊

I'll talk to you later 的口語說法

課文重點② Summary 2

A stable and long-lasting business relationship is always an important KPI for either a salesperson or a purchaser. In such a case, both the seller and the buyer benefit and grow together. In the long run, business negotiations, including price negotiation, become easier to conclude. In practice , to pursue consistent orders, more and more manufacturers are willing to offer timely incentive in the form of year-end volume rebate to their customers.

倘若生意規模由小至大持續成長，買賣雙方又能長期穩定配合，這種情況往往是買賣雙方最樂於見到的。由於購買量增加，賣方除了較能在售價上做彈性考量外，長期穩定的訂單，更讓賣方願意提供買方適時、適當的回饋，通常在年底以回扣方式為之。

議價 2　Price Negotiation 2　3-2

> **Sam** : **Purchaser, Adventure Computer (Singapore)** 採購
>
> **Christine** : **Sales Rep, Umax Inc. (Taiwan)** 業務代表

Sam : Hello Christine, this is Sam Martin, purchaser of Adventure Computer. How are you doing?

嗨 Christine，我是 Adventure Computer 的採購 Sam Martin。妳好嗎？

Christine : Pretty good, Sam. Thanks a lot. About increasing the quantity, do you have any good news?

還不錯，Sam，謝謝。關於增加採購數量，有沒有好消息？

Sam : Yes. Our customer agreed to increase the quantity to 20 units. What will be the discount?

有好消息給你。我們客戶答應買 20 臺，這樣的折扣是多少？

Christine : Great, my boss also agreed to a 10% discount for such quantity.

那太好了，我老闆也同意給你們 20 臺 10% 折扣。

Sam : Thanks for your help. And if we continue to buy from you in the future, will we get any rebate?

多謝幫忙。如果往後我們持續向你們購買的話，會有退佣嗎？

Christine : Yes, we do offer year-end volume rebate to qualified customers.

有的，我們提供給符合資格的客戶年終數量回扣。

Sam : Would you please explain in detail?

妳能說得更詳細些嗎？

Christine: By the end of the year, for any purchasing amount exceeding five hundred thousand dollars, you'll get 5% rebate.

到今年底，你們總出貨金額超過 50 萬元的部分，將會得到 5% 的回扣。

Sam: It sounds simple and clear, thanks for your explanations.

聽起來簡單清楚，謝謝妳的解釋。

Christine: No problem at all. When are you going to send me your P. O.?

小事一樁，別客氣。你哪時能傳給我訂單？

Sam: You'll receive it latest by 17:00 today.

最晚今天下午五點妳就能收到。

Christine: I appreciate it, good-bye.

謝謝，再見。

NOTE

1 stable：穩定的、安定的

Andy is good at maintaining a long-term stable relationship with customers by way of providing timely services to them.

藉著即時提供客戶所需服務，Andy 對於維持長期穩定的客戶關係非常在行。

② long-lasting：長期的、持久的

Establishing stable and long-lasting relationships with the key accounts has always been one of the KPIs for a B2B salesperson.

長久以來，與大客戶建立持久穩固的關係，一直是 B2B 業務人員的 KPI 之一。

③ KPI：重要績效指標

Key Performance Indicators 的縮寫

We do KPI evaluation for salespeople on a quarterly basis.

我們每季度都做業務人員的 KPI 評核。

④ either … or …：不是…就是…

Either Richard or Mark will have to show up at the conference tomorrow morning.

若不是 Richard 就是 Mark 得現身參加明早的大會。

⑤ purchaser：採購人員

Sharon has been a very picky purchaser for so many years.

這麼多年來，Sharon 一直是一位很挑剔的採購人員。

⑥ in such a case：在這情況下

In such a case, we will be forced to stop buying from you.

在這情況下，我們將不得不停止向你們採購。

NOTE

⑦ both … and …：…和…二者

Both Nancy and Rex are senior salespeople.

Nancy 和 Rex 二人都是資深業務人員。

當否定句型（二者均不是）時，須用 "neither … nor …" 表示，而不是直接否定

Neither Nancy nor Rex is a senior salesperson.

Nancy 和 Rex 都不是資深業務人員。

⑧ benefit：對…有利、對…有益、得利

Establishing mutual trust will benefit both the buyer and the seller.

建立互信對買賣雙方都有益。

⑨ grow：成長

To grow with your customers is a better way to secure their long-term business.

隨著客戶一起成長是確保長期生意的一種好方法。

⑩ in the long run：長期來看、終究

Definitely material costs are getting higher and higher in the long run.

長期來看，原料成本絕對會越來越高。

⑪ negotiation：協商、協調

We finally reached a conclusion on pricing through negotiations.

透過協商我們終於在價格上得到結論。

⑫ conclude：做最後決定或結論

Jerry concludes that from now on we should focus more on the tier one and tier two markets.

Jerry 做了最後決定，我們得更專注在第一階與第二階市場。

⑬ in practice：實際上、實務上

In practice, there are exceptions concerning payment.

關於付款，在實務上還是有例外的。

⑭ pursue：追求

It's very common for young salespeople to pursue higher income as their career goal.

對年輕業務人員來說，把追求高所得作為職涯目標是很常見的。

⑮ consistent：一致的

Lisa has been very consistent in her performance in the past 5 years.

過去 5 年來，Lisa 的表現都相當一致。

⑯ be willing to：願意

Definitely we are willing to work together with you to win the project.

我們當然願意和你們一起努力贏得這個案子。

NOTE

⑰ **timely**：及時的、適時的

The timely assistance from our FAE saves our customer from being penalized by the end customer.

我們 FAE 及時的協助，讓客戶躲過被終端客戶罰款的災難。

⑱ **incentive**：誘因、激勵、動力

Sales commission is always an important incentive to salespeople.

對業務人員來說，銷售佣金一直是一項重要的工作誘因。

⑲ **in the form of**：以…形式

The team will be rewarded by the company in the form of an overseas trip.

公司將以海外旅遊形式獎勵我們團隊。

⑳ **year-end volume rebate**：年終（結算）數量回扣

We're going to calculate the year-end volume rebate for you next week.

下星期我們將計算出要退給你們的年終數量回扣。

㉑ **pretty good**：很好、相當好，常用在口語

It feels pretty good to know the customer is pleased with my service.

知道客戶對我的服務表示滿意，感覺很開心。

NOTE

㉒ **about**：關於

About your recent RFQ, we will respond in an hour.

關於你們最近的 RFQ，我們會在一小時內回覆。

㉓ **agree to**：同意

對人或人的意見表示同意時，多半用 agree with

I agree with you that salespeople must be motivated to perform better.

我贊同你所說的，我們必須激勵業務人員表現得更好。

㉔ **discount**：折扣

Being one of our strategic channel partners, you deserve a better discount like this.

身為我們策略性通路夥伴之一，你們應該拿到更好的折扣。

㉕ **continue to**：持續、繼續

As expected, we continue to grow in the automation segment.

正如預期，我們持續在自動化區塊成長。

㉖ **rebate**：回扣

Offering a rebate is a general practice when doing business with EMS.

和 EMS 做生意，提供回扣是一種慣例做法。

㉗ **qualified**：符合資格的

She is qualified for receiving financial aid from the college.

她有資格拿到大學獎學金。

NOTE

㉘ **explain in detail**：詳細解釋

The application is quite sophisticated. You'd better explain in detail.

這是個很複雜的應用，你得詳細解釋才行。

㉙ **by the end of the year**：到年底時

I'm confident that we'll be able to come up with the samples you need by the end of the year.

我有信心到年底時，我們有辦法提供你們所需的樣品。

㉚ **exceed**：超過、超出

Team's Y-T-D sales reached $25M, exceeding our target by 20%.

我們團隊的 Y-T-D 營收已達到 2500 萬美金，超出我們的目標 20%。

㉛ **it sounds**：聽起來

It sounds weird.

聽起來很怪異。

㉜ **latest by**：最遲至

Don't worry, I'll hand in my report latest by Friday.

別擔心，我最晚會在週五交出報告的。

 **Summary 3**

An introduction to EMS way of price negotiation:
EMS firms conduct a systematic price negotiation with each and every vendor to ensure everything is in good order with the entire supply chain. A quarterly or biannual price review meeting is called and held by the sourcing personnel. During the meeting, existing prices and order allocations are reviewed on one hand and new prices and allocations for the following period are discussed and negotiated on the other. The only purpose of the meeting is to keep the purchasing prices under control through their tremendous bargaining power, namely, the enormous business volume on hand.

The salesperson who attends the review meeting must act carefully and properly, according to pre-calculated data provided by relevant departments such as operations, costing or finance, and product marketing. Moreover, it is of vital importance that salespersons deal with both the sourcer and the purchaser in a nice and smooth way as they are the final gatekeepers and decision makers prior to releasing purchase orders.

EMS 電子製造服務代工廠議價方式簡介：

EMS 物料搜尋主管或採購主管，定期與廠商業務人員逐一進行議價談判，每次會議主題大同小異，較少有臨時動議的情形。因此雙方都能在會議之前做好充分準備，好在現場做出最適當的決策。以下對話內容，涵蓋了兩種最常見的會議對話。

特別是在消費性電子產業裡，EMS 廠或 OEM 廠，大多會要求零組件供應廠，派代表參加每半年（甚至每季度）一次的售價檢討會議，目的在於持續壓低零組件價格；而所依賴的，就是手中大量的訂單。由於 EMS 廠零組件供應商眾多，同一料件往往有好幾家供應商。EMS 會按照競爭性高低，分配各家下單比例，這就是所謂配額，採購就依循比例下單。然而在實際操作上，由於需求量與交期等因素時時在變化，採購人員還是會依照實際狀況彈性做調整，仍然握有相當大的下單權力。也因此這種定期議價的場合，對業務人員來說就非常重要了。除了會前必須充分準備，根據內部相關單位所提供數據於會議中謹慎行事外，對於搜尋人員和採購都要趁機打好關係，全是為了訂單。

 EMS 議價   EMS Price Negotiation   3-3

 : Sourcing Manager, Global Luke (EMS, Singapore)
Frank   搜尋經理

 : Deputy Sales Manager, Q-Tecs (Taiwan) 業務副理
Denise   **Denise attends meeting.** Denise 前來 EMS 參加會議

 : Hi Denise, <u>how's it going</u>? Welcome to the meeting. I hope
Frank   you have prepared well so that we may finish the meeting in
two hours.

嗨！Denise，你好嗎？歡迎你來開會。我希望你都準備好了，
以便讓會議能在兩小時內結束。

這類會議講求效率，事前做足準備非常重要。

 : Just great, thanks. Yes, I'm ready for the meeting.
Denise   我很好，謝謝。是的，我準備好了。

 : OK, let's <u>review</u> the existing situation <u>one by one</u>. With our
Frank   X5552, among four current <u>vendors</u>, you're given 18% of our
business. You're not very competitive.

好，我們就逐項來看現在的情形，先看我們 X5552 這顆料好
了。在四家供應商裡，你們分到 18% 的量，競爭力不太好喔。

Dr. Lee 解析

議價品項可能有多項，會先逐一檢視現狀，包括現有售價與訂單配額。

Denise: I know. We'll be more aggressive on this item by matching competitors' price. We are shooting at 25% of your business.

我知道。針對這顆料，我們會更積極地跟進對手的價格，目標是拿到你們 25% 的生意量。

Dr. Lee 解析

供應廠商對品項 X5552 未來半年的態度與期望是：加入價格戰，目標拿下 25% 的 EMS 訂單量。

Frank: I don't think matching alone will help you get any more business as all others are doing the same. Meanwhile, don't forget that you still have a capacity problem.

由於每家供應廠都會這麼做，我不認為你們單單拼價格就能多拿到生意。而且，別忘了你們還有產能問題。

Dr. Lee 解析

EMS 絕對會在供應商之間耍手段殺價錢。另外，產能重要性被提出。

Denise: I'm just about to tell you that we have solved the capacity problem already. We set up a new line in Shanghai last month and that is designated for your X5552.

我正要告訴你，我們的產能問題已經解決了。上個月，我們在上海新開了一條生產線，專門生產 X5552。

Dr. Lee 解析

供應商表示早先產能不足問題已經解決，這條新產線是專屬 X5552 的生產線，針對性很明顯。

Frank: Well, that is a plus and we'll take it into consideration. Now, let's see Z8783. With your existing price, you have been given some 12% of our business. Again, the item will become much tougher for you.

那倒是一項加分，我們也會將此列入考慮。現在來看看 Z8783 這顆料。以你們現在的價格，大約分到 12% 的生意量。同樣的，這顆料對你們來說會更加吃力吧？

Dr. Lee 解析

Sourcer 再繼續針對其它不同品項的價格施壓，並且明白表示想多拿生意就得降價。

Denise: True. With such pricing, we seem to be out of competition for this item. However, we can't afford to lose any of this business considering its quantity. Therefore, we are expecting to <u>maintain</u> the current share for the next 6 months.

確實如此。以這樣的售價來看，這顆料我們似乎無法競爭。不過考慮到這顆料的量，我們不想丟掉任何訂單。所以，我們希望在未來半年裡，能維持住目前的配額比例。

Dr. Lee 解析

算盤大家都會打，在這裡，供應廠商表明立場，希望保持現有配額就好。然而事情往往沒這麼簡單。

Frank：For this <u>commodity item</u>, price and capacity are what we <u>concern</u> the most. If you want to maintain the <u>allocation</u>, you'll have to <u>compete head-on with</u> all other bigger vendors.

這種大宗貨物，我們最在意的就是價格和產能。如果你們想要維持配額，就一定得和其他大廠硬碰硬競爭才行。

Dr. Lee 解析

「commodity item」是指量大低售價的大宗項目，比的就是價格與產能，缺一不可。果不其然，sourcer 講明 Q-Tecs 在這二項指標上都佔不到便宜。

Denise：I understand. <u>I need a favor from you.</u> <u>Off the records</u>, <u>do you mind telling me</u> how I should quote today to be able to keep the allocation for Z8783?

我了解。我需要你幫忙，這不列入會議記錄哦！你介不介意指點我該如何，我應該如何報價來保住 Z8783 的配額呢？

Dr. Lee 解析

可看出業務與對方主事者之間關係相當深厚，能在現場提出如此敏感的要求。「Off the records」是指這段交談不列入會議紀錄。

Frank : You know my position very well. I'm not supposed to give you any specific numbers, yet, I'll give you this range to consider (writing down on a piece of memo).
你很清楚我的立場啊！我無法給你一個確切數字，不過這個範圍讓你參考（寫在便條紙上）。

Dr. Lee 解析

EMS 為求本身利益，會打間諜牌，軟硬兼施，要供應商就範。

Denise : Thanks very much. So, I need to hand in my price proposal in an hour?
多謝你啦！我是不是要在一小時內把報價提案交給你？

Frank : Yes, please. I'll be back in 50 minutes.
是的，我過 50 分鐘再回來。

Dr. Lee 解析

大多 EMS 講求高效率，開會就要求能定案。

NOTE

❶ EMS：電子製造服務代工廠

Electronics Manufacturing Services 的縮寫。現今知名 EMS 如富士康 Foxconn、偉創力 Flextronics、捷普 Jabil 和新美亞 Sanmina-SCI

❷ conduct：實施、進行、執行

We will conduct an all-out sales campaign in order to sell more of our new sensors in Q4.

為了要在 Q4 裡多賣出新型感應器，我們會進行一次全員出動的銷售活動。

❸ systematic：有系統的

In order to improve work efficiency, we started to run systematic on-job training for all salespeople.

為了改善工作效率，我們開始對全體業務同仁進行系統化的在職訓練。

❹ vendor：供應廠商

Lynx Tire doesn't put all its eggs into just one basket. It has at least two vendors for each key component it buys.

Lynx Tire 並沒有將所有雞蛋都放在同一籃子裡，他們每一項關鍵零組件至少會找二家供應商。

NOTE

⑤ ensure：確保、保證

We need to ensure our customers that the fire won't affect our delivery schedule.

我們得對客戶保證，火災將不影響我們交期。

⑥ in good order：沒問題、有條不紊、情況正常

To make sure everything is in good order, would you please confirm with the supplier one more time?

為了要確保一切都沒問題，能否麻煩你和供應廠商再確認一次好嗎？

⑦ entire：整個、完全的

The entire sales team was very excited because of the outstanding Q3 performance.

因為第三季的表現非常突出，整個業務團隊感到興奮異常。

⑧ supply chain：供應鏈

Fox Machinery has built up a strong and supportive supply chain in recent years.

Fox Machinery 在近幾年內打造了一條強大穩固的供應鏈。

⑨ quarterly：每季的、每年四次的

We are reviewing the performance of our salespeople on a quarterly basis.

我們每季檢討一次業務人員的工作績效。

NOTE

⑩ biannual：每年二次的

Our applications seminar is being held on a biannual basis.
我們的應用研討會每年舉辦二次。

⑪ call：召開

We will call a global sales meeting through video conference next week.
我們將在下週透過視訊會議召開全球業務會議。

⑫ hold：舉行、為（了）…

An R&D conference with Sun Automation on instruments selection will be held on Friday morning.
星期五上午我們與 Sun Automation 舉行一場有關儀器選擇的研發討論會。

Jeff is being held responsible for the launch of G4 smartphone.
Jeff 得為我們的 G4 智慧型手機上市負責。

⑬ sourcing personnel：（物料）搜尋人員

多半稱為 sourcer，隸屬採購部門，有不少物料工程師出身

Many purchasing centers consist of both sourcing and purchasing personnel.
許多採購中心是由搜尋人員與採購人員組成。

NOTE

⑭ **allocation**：配額

I believe Toyo Denki is going to fill up its allocation by the end of Q3.

我相信 Toyo Denki 將會在第三季底填滿他們的配額。

⑮ **review**：檢討、檢視

My boss is going to review my Q2 performance face to face tomorrow.

我老闆明天要面對面檢討我第二季的業績。

⑯ **on one hand … on the other**：一方面…另一方面

A B2B salesperson represents the company communicating with the customer on one hand and represents the customer communicating with many internal departments of the company on the other.

一位 B2B 業務人員一方面代表公司與客戶溝通，另一方面也代表客戶和公司內部許多部門溝通。

⑰ **keep … under control**：使…在掌控之中

As the industry leader, we work very hard to keep market order under control.

身為產業龍頭老大，我們非常努力地掌控市場秩序。

⑱ **tremendous**：極大的、巨大的

Our team has been under tremendous pressure to achieve a 200% growth target of sales revenue.

NOTE

我們業務團隊為了要達成一項 200% 的營收成長目標，承受了極大的壓力。

⑲ **bargaining power**：議價能力

A large EMS always has more bargaining power doing business with components manufacturers.

在和零組件廠商打交道時，大型 EMS 一向有更強的議價能力。

⑳ **namely**：亦即、也就是、換句話說

We have a very unique competitive advantage, namely our local applications support.

我們擁有一項非常獨特的競爭優勢，那就是在地應用支援。

㉑ **enormous**：極大的、巨大的

Sometimes voluminous orders from EMS customers create enormous pressures to us.

有時候來自 EMS 的大單會帶給我們極大壓力。

㉒ **attend**：參加、出席

All of our R&D engineers and our FAEs will attend the technical seminar.

我們所有的研發工程師和應用工程師都會參加這次技術研討會。

NOTE

㉓ act：行動、動作、作為

Despite the setback in pursuing the project business, we acted decently and won respect from our customer.

儘管在爭取專案訂單遭受挫敗，我們舉止有度還是贏得客戶的尊敬。

㉔ properly：恰當地、正確地

Sandy responded properly to the customer rejecting its unreasonable requests.

Sandy 回應得很恰當，拒絕了客戶的無理要求。

㉕ pre-calculated：事前計算好的

I've got all the pre-calculated data on hand and I'm going to meet my boss.

我帶著所有事先算好的數據去找老闆開會。

㉖ relevant：相關的、相對應的

Please pass on the notice to all relevant parties.

請將這份通知傳給所有相關人員。

㉗ operations：作業、運籌

Negotiating with operations department is what we salespeople frequently do every day.

與營運部門協調是我們業務人員每天經常在做的事。

㉘ costing：成本計算

As to what we should quote, you will have to ask the costing department.

NOTE

至於我們該報什麼價格，你得去問成本部門。

㉙ finance：財務

It's no exception. Our finance department is very strict with money.
不例外，我們財務部門對錢很嚴格。

㉚ product marketing：產品行銷

With regard to the trade shows in the coming year, our product marketing manager will give you a briefing.
有關明年度參展，我們的產品行銷經理會向你簡報。

㉛ moreover：而且、此外

Moreover, we'll offer you VMI service.
此外，我們還會提供 VMI 服務。

㉜ it is of vital importance：極為重要

It is of vital importance that salespeople sync up with PM for the ongoing projects on a regular basis.
業務人員定期與 PM 針對進行中專案溝通極為重要。

㉝ deal with：處理、對付

We have a systematic way to deal with returns.
我們有一套制度化的方法處理退貨。

㉞ in a nice and smooth way：以一種友善圓滿的方式

Concerning their complaint last week, we resolved it in a nice and smooth way.

NOTE

關於上星期他們的客訴，我們已經用友善圓滿的方式解決了。

㉟ gatekeeper：把關者

Being the final gatekeeper, finance department will always play tough.

身為最後把關單位，財務部門一向很強悍。

㊱ decision maker：做決策者

Most of the time, product manager and R&D engineer are the final decision makers.

產品經理和研發工程師多半都是最後決策者。

㊲ prior to：在…之前

Prior to departure, salespeople need to make sure the updated itinerary has been distributed to all parties concerned.

出發之前，業務得確定最新的日程已經分發給每一相關人員。

㊳ release purchase orders：開出訂單

Please make sure the purchaser releases purchase orders according to the meeting conclusions.

請務必確定採購依照會議結論開出訂單。

㊴ how's it going?：你好嗎？

這適用於平輩而且有一定交情的對象，否則還是得使用較為傳統有禮的 How are you? *或是* How are you doing?

㊵ review：檢討、檢視

Vicky, let's review what you proposed.

Vicky，我們一起看看你的提案吧！

NOTE

㊶ one by one：逐一、一個個

In the meeting, we discussed and resolved all the issues one by one.

會議中，我們逐一討論並解決所有問題。

㊷ vendor：供應廠商，也可說 suppliers

㊸ aggressive：積極有作為、具侵略性

Ruby, you have to be more aggressive with those strategic accounts.

Ruby，對那些策略性客戶你得更積極才行。

㊹ match competitors' price：跟價格

比方說，供應商甲的報價是 @$50，若供應商乙原本想報 @$60，為了要做成生意，也跟進改報 @$50

We were forced to match competitors' price this time.

這一回我們不得不跟進競爭對手的價格了。

㊺ shoot at 25%：瞄準目標 25%

For this project, we're shooting at 25% profitability.

對於這個案子，我們的利潤目標是 25%。

㊻ help you get：幫你得到

不用 help you to get，現在口說英語的習慣用法

Don't worry. I'll help you get enough food and snacks for the long weekend.

別擔心，我會幫你買到足夠的食物和零嘴度過長週末。

NOTE

㊼ meanwhile：同時、在同一時間內，也可說**in the meantime**

Dave finally got the order. Meanwhile, all his colleagues in the office were keeping their fingers crossed.

Dave 終於拿到訂單了！在此同時，所有辦公室的同事都在祝他好運。

㊽ capacity：產能、容量、能力

Jim, what's your maximum capacity of TC003?

Jim，你們 TC003 的最大產能是多少？

㊾ solve：解決

Now I'm asking you to solve your customer's application problems immediately.

我要求你現在立即解決客戶在應用上的問題。

㊿ set up a new line：設立起一條新產線

(51) is designated for：被指定為、被指派為

All these new CNC machines are designated for Dyson's smartwatches.

這些新 CNC 加工機全都是專門用來生產 Dyson's 的智慧手錶。

NOTE

52 plus：加分的項目

When we're reviewing applicant's qualifications, experience in relevant industries is definitely a plus.

當我們在審閱應徵者資歷時，相關產業經驗必定是加分項目。

53 take it into consideration：列入考慮

Regarding the market information previously provided by you, we will take it into consideration while we're making our final decision.

關於你先前提供的市場資訊，我們會在做最後決定時列入考慮。

54 existing：現有的、現成的

55 out of competition：失去競爭力

I'm sorry, Ian. If we fail to come up with an effective marketing strategy, we'll be out of competition very soon.

抱歉，Ian。如果我們無法提出一套有效的行銷策略，很快就會失去競爭力。

56 can't afford to：承擔不起、負擔不起

We can't afford to lose such a strategic account like M Systems.

我們承擔不起失去像 M Systems 這樣一家策略性客戶。

NOTE

(57) **consider**：考量、看在…份上

Ok, I agree to do it on one-off basis, considering their past contribution to us.

好吧！看在他們過去對公司的貢獻，我同意這麼去做，但就僅僅這一次。

(58) **maintain**：維持、保持

We are determined to maintain our leading position in the market as we committed before.

如同我們先前所承諾，我們有決心維持市場龍頭老大的地位。

(59) **commodity item**：大宗貨物，意指市場需求量特別大的項目

Hey, listen up! These rock-bottom prices are for commodity items only.

嘿！大家聽好了。這些低到不行的價格只適用在大宗貨物上啊！

(60) **concern**：擔心、關心

What we concern the most is whether our offerings are competitive enough or not.

我們最擔心的是，到底我們的提案競爭力是否夠強。

NOTE

61 allocation：配額

Frank, we need more orders from you in Q3 as we still have plenty of open allocation on hand.

Frank，第三季你得多丟些訂單給我們，因為我們手上還有很多空配額。

62 compete head-on with：正面競爭、直接競爭

For such a commodity item, we will have to compete head-on with our competitors.

對這種大宗貨物的生意，我們只能正面迎戰了。

63 I need a favor from you.：我需要你幫忙。

64 off the records：不列入會議紀錄，意指私底下的談話

OK, off the records and just between you and me. You won the tender.

好，這不列入紀錄，只有我們兩個知道：你們拿到標案了。

65 do you mind telling me：你介意告訴我嗎

mind 後面要接動名詞形式，所以「告訴」這動詞要用 telling

Do you mind telling me the applications you're referring to?

你介不介意告訴我，你所指的應用是什麼？

66 I'm not supposed to：我不應該、我不可以

I'm sorry, Grace. I'm not supposed to comment on it.

對不起，Grace，這點我不該去評論。

NOTE

67 specific：具體的、特定的

68 range：範圍

We are selling a wide range of machine tools in Australia.

我們在澳洲販賣很多種類的機床。

69 write down：寫下

Tom, please write down what Mark has just told us on the white board.

Tom，請你把剛才 Mark 告訴我們的內容寫在白板上。

70 hand in：交出、提出

Don't worry, Hans. I'll be able to hand in my report in time next Monday.

Hans 別擔心，我下週一會及時交出報告的。

71 proposal：提案、提議

An effective proposal on sales strategy has to be constructive and realistic.

一份有效的銷售策略提案一定要有建設性，而且還要夠實際才行。

Lesson 4　下單 - 交期
P.O. : O.A. & Delivery

 Summary 1

After receiving the <u>purchase order</u>, the supplier will <u>review</u> the P.O. and send an <u>order acknowledgment</u> (O.A.) to the buyer. The O.A. <u>serves as</u> the final <u>formal document</u> <u>based on</u> which the purchase order is accepted and processed. <u>Very often</u>, the terms <u>shown</u> on the O.A. <u>differ from</u> those shown on purchase order <u>as a result of</u> the <u>compromises</u> made by <u>the two parties</u> <u>through</u> <u>negotiation</u>. The buyer will have to <u>endorse</u> it and send it back to the supplier. Just like the RFQ, O.A. is also one of the most important <u>commercial documents</u> in a business <u>transaction</u>. The <u>consequence</u> of <u>overlooking</u> it could be <u>devastating</u>.

供應商在收到訂單後，會依照自身生產條件，儘可能滿足訂單需求，並製作訂單確認書。訂單確認書也被視為商業交易訂單處理中最終的正式文件。經由買賣雙方的協商，訂單確認書上的交易條件，往往和訂單上的相關條件有所差異。在接獲訂單確認書後，買方客戶必須簽字表示接受，並回傳給賣方供應商。正如同 RFQ，訂單確認書是商業交易中最重要的商業文件之一，買賣雙方都須格外注意避免出錯。

下單—交期 P.O.：Delivery 4-1

 Sam ： **Purchaser, Adventure Computer (Singapore)** 採購

Christine ： **Sales Rep, Umax Inc. (Taiwan)** 業務代表

Sam： Hi Christine, this is Sam Martin from Adventure Computer. How are you doing today?

嗨 Christine，我是 Adventure Computer 的 Sam Martin。妳今天好嗎？

Christine： Fine, thanks. How may I help you, Sam?

謝謝你，Sam，我很好。有什麼我能替你服務的嗎？

Sam： I received your order acknowledgment, but I have a question about delivery.

我收到妳傳來的訂單確認了，但我對交期有些疑問。

Christine： OK, what is it?

是喔，什麼疑問？

Sam： An 8-week lead time is too long. We need to receive the goods in 4 weeks.

8 週太長了。我們必須在 4 週內收到貨。

Christine： Is it so? Eight weeks is our standard lead time. Our production lines are very busy.

是喔？8 週是我們一般的標準交期，現在生產線太忙了。

Sam： We need the machines badly. We've got to receive them in four weeks.

我們非得在 4 週內收到這些機器。

Christine : OK, let me check with our planner to see if it's possible to shorten the lead time. I'll call you back once I'm done.

我來和生管討論一下，看看是否能縮短交期。等會兒確認了再回覆你。

Sam : Thanks very much.

多謝了。

(later...)

Christine : Hi Sam, good news, we will ship the machines in 30 days.

嗨 Sam，好消息！我們可在 30 天內出貨。

Sam : That's great, thanks a lot. You've been very helpful.

那太棒了，謝謝你。妳真的幫了大忙。

Christine : I'm really happy things worked out well.

能順利提前，我也很高興。

❶ **purchase order**：訂單，簡稱P.O.

❷ **review**：檢視、檢查、考核

As a sales head, I have to review all kinds of reports prepared by the salespeople in the ERP system.

身為業務主管，我得在 ERP 系統上檢視業務人員所製作的各式報告。

NOTE

We do the performance review for each salesperson on a biannual basis.

每半年我們就對每位業務人員做一次績效考核。

❸ order acknowledgment：訂單確認

縮寫為 O.A.，也常見用 Order Confirmation。是接單廠商在完成訂單處理後，對下單客戶發出 O.A.。裡面記載該份訂單各項履行條件，以作為買賣雙方共同依循的根據

❹ serve as：作為、當作

The mail serves as the shipping notice of your recent Order No. MA200419.

這封郵件作為你們最近一張訂單編號 MA200419 的出貨通知。

❺ formal：正式的

Instead of quoting by e-mail, please send your formal quotation to me asap.

請儘快傳給我你們正式的報價單，不要用 e-mail 報價。

❻ document：文件

Salespeople must pay close attention to the legal documents such as the Supply Agreement.

業務人員必須特別留意法律文件，比如供貨協議。

7 based on：根據、以…為基礎

Based on the Y-T-D shipment record, we would foresee a significant growth of Acron's business by the end of the year.

根據今年目前為止的出貨紀錄，我們能預見到今年底 Acron 的生意將有顯著的成長。

Y-T-D 是 Year-To-Date 的縮寫

8 very often：經常、時常

Very often salespeople fail to get along with marketing people.

業務人員經常與行銷人員處不來。

9 show：顯示、表示

The figures shown on this row of the budget spreadsheet are the sales target of each month next year.

在預算試算表這一行裡的數字，就是明年每個月的銷售目標。

10 differ from：不同於

Because of his seniority, my expectation toward Charles differs from that of others.

由於 Charles 比較資深，我對他的期望不同於其他人。

11 as a result of：由於、因此

As a result of the shipping delay, we were forced to shut down the production lines for 6 hours.

由於運輸延遲，我們被迫將生產線關機 6 小時。

NOTE

⑫ **compromise**：妥協、讓步

In order to close the deal quicker, Don made compromises on pricing with the customer.

為了快點結案拿到訂單，Don 在價格上對客戶做了讓步。

⑬ **the two parties**：指買賣雙方

⑭ **through**：藉由、經由、經過

Through continuous negotiation, the two companies agreed to settle the case out of the court.

經由不斷地協商，這二家公司同意庭外和解。

⑮ **negotiation**：協商、談判、協調

Salespeople should be equipped with good negotiation skills.

業務人員應該具備良好的協商技巧。

⑯ **endorse**：背書、核准、簽名、贊同

I would endorse Stacy's decision to drop the deal because it will keep us away from trouble.

我贊同 Stacy 做出放棄那訂單的決定，因為那樣會讓我們少掉很多麻煩。

⑰ **commercial documents**：商業文件

⑱ transaction：交易

From time to time, salespeople make mistakes in some complicated transactions.

業務人員不時會在複雜的交易中犯錯。

⑲ consequence：後果、結果

The consequence of a poor business decision can be tremendous.

一個糟糕的業務決策會產生非常嚴重的後果。

⑳ overlook：忽視、輕忽

Overlooking the importance of customer service can be extremely dangerous.

輕忽客服的重要性是非常危險的。

㉑ devastating：殺傷力強大的、恐怖具毀滅性的

Sometimes competing by undercutting others can be so devastating that everybody loses.

有時候用降價搶單來競爭會造成兩敗俱傷的慘劇。

㉒ delivery：交貨、出貨

Just like our selling price, delivery lead time is one of the most important competitive edges we offer to our customers.

就如同我們的售價，交期也是我們最重要的競爭優勢之一。

NOTE

㉓ **8-week**：8週的

用 8-week 來形容交期 lead time，而不說 8 weeks lead time，沒有發 S 的音

Our supplier gave us a 8-week transit time by sea freight. We asked them to use air freight instead.

我們的供應商給我們一個 8 週的海運期，我們要求改用空運。

㉔ **lead time**：交貨前置時間，與交期同義

We promised our customer to shorten our lead time by 2 weeks.

我們承諾客戶縮短交期二週。

㉕ **badly**：極度地、嚴重地

The consecutive recalls in recent months have badly hurt their reputation.

最近幾個月的連續召回，已經嚴重危害到他們的聲譽。

㉖ **we've got to**：我們必需，也可說We must …

We've got to find an effective way to take back those lost accounts, specifically tier-1 accounts.

我們必須想出有效的辦法來搶回流失的客戶，特別是第一階客戶。

NOTE

㉗ shorten：縮短，增長用**lengthen**

As per our request, the supplier shortened the lead time from 15 days to 12 days.

根據我們的要求，供應廠商縮短了交期，由 15 天縮短成 12 天。

㉘ I'll call you back once I'm done.：一旦好了我就給你回電。

Hey Dave, I am actually on another call right now. Can I call you back once I am done here?"

嘿，Dave，我正在講另一通電話，等我說完後回電好嗎？

㉙ you've been very helpful.：你幫了大忙。

Regarding selling price, you've been very helpful.

關於售價，你真是幫了大忙。

㉚ things worked out well：事情順利進行、問題順利解決

My boss was very happy to know that things worked out well.

對於事情能順利進行，我老闆很高興。

課文重點② Summary 2

From time to time, even after the O.A. is issued, the supplier would receive urgent request from the buyer customer asking for earlier delivery of part, if not all, of the products they ordered. In such a case, the supplier would try to pull in the delivery schedule. On other occasions, the buyer would ask the supplier to delay the delivery of part, if not all, of the order without any reasons. In such a case, the supplier will have to push out the original delivery schedule. In either case, the supplier will face certain pressures in terms of adjusting production plans. It will be a lot tougher to pull in urgent delivery under full-capacity operation. Pushing out delivery also results in higher inventory level and heavier financial burden.

然而，並非在OA確認後就一切太平。實際上，供應商不時會接到客戶要求緊急出貨。倘若是一階客戶，供應廠商多半會盡量設法滿足提前交貨要求。相反的，有時客戶也會要求延後交貨。無論提前或延後，都會對供應廠商帶來生產計畫上的壓力。尤其是在產線滿載的時候，要再提前交貨更是困難；而延後交貨則會造成成品庫存瞬間增加，公司資金壓力大增。

提前交貨 & 延後交貨　Pull-in & Push-out 4-2

Sam ：**Purchaser, Adventure Computer (Singapore)** 採購

Christine ：**Sales Rep, Umax Inc. (Taiwan)** 業務代表

Sam ： Hi Christine, this is Sam Martin from Adventure Computer, how's everything going?

嗨 Christine，我是 Adventure Computer 的 Sam Martin，你好嗎？

 Dr. Lee 解析

how's everything going 同 how's it going？

Christine ： Hi Sam, great, thanks. How about yourself?

嗨 Sam，我很好啊！謝謝。那你呢？

Dr. Lee 解析

用 great 表示很好，也能用 fine 或 very good。how about yourself？等同問 how're you doing？

Sam ： Very busy. Now I need a favor from you. We need you to pull in delivery of our order for YT2520 under your O.A. number MD997 and ship it to us in two days.

我超忙的。現在我得請妳幫個忙，我們想請妳把訂單確認書編號MD997，我們的訂單YT2520交期提前，並且在二日內交貨。

Dr. Lee 解析

通常，在 B2B 模式裡，賣方業務與買方採購之間，若是公事公辦，基本上就沒什麼 favor 可言。這句話裡，Sam 有求於 Christine，用了 I need a favor from you，可看出二者之間因業務往來建立起的依賴關係，可以直接請對方幫忙。

Christine：Just a minute, MD997? I'm <u>digging out</u> the details from our system. Now I see it. Wait a minute, Sam, you're asking me to <u>pull in</u> by one week?

請等一下，Sam，是 MD997 嗎？我現在就從系統裡找出來。
我看到了，等等，Sam，你是要我提前一週交貨？

Dr. Lee 解析

根據 Sam 提供的 O.A. 編號，Christine 當場直接由訂單系統叫出那張 O.A. 資料檢視。才發現 Sam 要求提前一週交貨。

Sam：Yes, we just received a request from our customer that we need to <u>urgently</u> deliver to them one week earlier than the <u>original</u> date.

是的。我們剛剛收到客戶要求，要我們比原交期提早一週，緊急出貨給他們。

Dr. Lee 解析

B2B 供應鏈經常會發生這種連鎖反應，最終客戶（Adventure 電腦公司的客戶）需求一旦改變，就會擴大影響到供應鏈源頭生產廠商（Umax 公司）的供貨計畫。

Christine: It will be very <u>tough</u> for us to pull in delivery <u>at the moment</u> as we have been <u>running at full capacity</u> in recent months. Pulling in your order would mean pushing out others'. I really <u>doubt</u> we'll be able to do it.

在這時候要我們提前交貨真的很困難。因為近幾個月來，我們產能都是滿載。要提前你們的訂單交期，就表示得延後其他客戶的交期。我真的很懷疑我們有辦法做到。

Dr. Lee 解析

倘若生產廠商（Umax）當時產能爆滿的話，要臨時大幅改變生產計劃，是非常困難的。若替 Adventure 插單，就勢必得延後其他客戶訂單履行，況且還會產生排程更動的成本。

Sam: I fully understand your situation. However, we'll be in a <u>shaky position</u> if we <u>fail to meet our customer's request</u>. I would <u>very much appreciate</u> your help <u>in this regard</u>.

我完全能理解妳的處境。不過要是沒法滿足客戶提前交貨的要求，我們會很慘的。如果妳能幫我們忙，我會非常感激的。

Dr. Lee 解析

> 這裡，Sam 向 Christine 說明提出提前交貨的背後，乃因為他們的最終客戶先臨時提出要求，要 Adventure 提前出貨。

Christine : OK, I'll see what we can do and get back to you later today.

好吧！我來設法看看。會在今天稍晚回覆你。

Dr. Lee 解析

> 基於彼此互助原則，Christine 同意會設法解決難題。

Sam : Thank you so much.

真是多謝妳啊！

(later...)

Christine : Hi Sam, about your pull-in request, I just came out from a lengthy meeting with a solution. However, it may not be exactly what you're looking for.

嗨！Sam，關於你們提前交貨的要求，我們才開完一次馬拉松協調會，想出一個解決方案，不過這可能和你期待的有所差異。

Dr. Lee 解析

> 在如此困難的情況下，供應廠商研商結果，通常無法完全滿足需求，不過還是有改善的。

Sam ： OK, what's the solution?

好，是怎樣的解決方案呢？

Dr. Lee 解析

Sam 迫不及待想知道詳情。

Christine ： We'll be able to pull in 250,000 units <u>the day after tomorrow</u> and another 250,000 units two more days later. The <u>remaining</u> 500,000 units will be delivered to you <u>according to</u> our original schedule.

我們有辦法提前在後天先出25萬片，過二天之後再出25萬片。剩下的 50 萬片，則按照原定交期出貨。

Dr. Lee 解析

供應廠商 Umax 解決方案，至少能解決客戶 Adventure50% 的緊急問題；剩下的由客戶與其最終客戶協商解決。

Sam ： I guess it's <u>the best you can do,</u> <u>isn't it?</u>

我想你們已經盡全力了，是吧？

Dr. Lee 解析

Sam 心知肚明，廠商已盡力。

Christine: Yes, it is. We do understand your situation. However, <u>switching</u> production capacity <u>abruptly</u> is always difficult while the capacity is full.

是的，我們確實盡力了。我們很清楚你們的處境。不過當產線滿載，又要臨時抽換產能，確實非常困難。

Dr. Lee 解析

站在供應商立場，Christine 再次向 Sam 強調，臨時更動的困難度很高。

Sam: I really appreciate your efforts. <u>In such a case</u>, I believe we'll <u>be able to</u> deliver 50% of what we were requested to supply next week. And I'm sure our customer will be happy about it.

你們這麼幫忙，我真的很感激。在這情況下，我們就有辦法在下星期內出給客戶所要求 50% 的貨。我客戶肯定會很高興的。

Dr. Lee 解析

問題幾乎能馬上解決一半，Sam 當然高興，也對於能說服其最終用戶保有信心。

Christine: <u>Sounds good</u>, I'll send the <u>revised</u> delivery plan to you <u>right away</u>.

聽起來不錯喔！我會馬上把新的交貨細節傳給你。

Dr. Lee 解析

口說無憑，一切都得靠最後書面文字。

☺ ： Again, thanks so much. You've been so <u>supportive</u>.
Sam
再次謝謝妳喔！妳一直都那麼幫忙。

Dr. Lee 解析

一定得道謝。

☺ ： No problem. I'm glad things <u>work out well</u> for both of us.
Christine
不客氣。我也很高興能有雙贏的結果。

Dr. Lee 解析

能夠有雙贏結果很讚。

NOTE

❶ from time to time：不時、經常

From time to time, we salespeople run into some unexpected trouble that would ruin our mood entirely.

我們業務人員不時會碰上一些意料不到的麻煩事，使整個心情大壞。

❷ even：甚至、即使

Even now, after leaving my previous employer for so many years, some old-time customers still buzz me from time to time.

即使到現在，離開前東家多年之後，有些昔日客戶還是不時來電找我。

I think we'd better stop discussing as we don't even have a consensus about the crisis we're facing.

我認為我們應該停止討論，因為我們甚至對眼前面臨的危機都沒有共識。

even 用在否定句形時都是緊跟在 not 之後

❸ issue：開立、開出、發出

Jim, since you already agreed on the revised unit price, would you please issue the P.O. as soon as possible?

Jim，既然你也同意我們修正過後的單價，能否請你儘快開訂單呢？

❹ if not all：即使不是全部

I guess most, if not all, of our customers are not happy that we implemented general rate increase on such a short notice.

NOTE

即使不是全部，我估計多數客戶對我們臨時通知實施全面漲價會很不高興。

⑤ in such a case：在這種情況下

In such a case, we will have to meet customer's request and offer the same price as the competitor's.

在這種情況下，我們也只能滿足客戶要求，跟進競爭同行的價格。

⑥ pull in the delivery schedule：提前出貨

The supplier agreed to pull in the delivery schedule of our order TX07001 by 5 days.

供應廠商同意將我們的訂單 TX07001 提前 5 天出貨。

⑦ on other occasions：在其他時候

Our global sales teams meet face to face on a regular basis. On other occasions, if necessary, we discuss via video conference.

我們在世界各地的業務團隊會定期碰頭開會，而在其他必要的時候也會用視訊會議來討論。

⑧ without：沒有、無、不用

They canceled the order without giving us any explanations.

他們沒做任何解釋就取消訂單了。

It goes without saying that we must beat the competition and win back those lost accounts.

我們當然得戰勝對手，並把流失的客戶搶回來。

NOTE

⑨ push out the original delivery schedule：
延後出貨

Because of the unexpected demand drop in recent months, we'll have to ask our suppliers to push out the original delivery schedule.

由於近月來需求意外滑落，我們得要求供應廠商延後出貨。

⑩ in either case：（兩種情況中）無論哪一種情況

In either case, you'll find our solution a much better choice.

無論哪一種情況，你會發現我們的解決方案是更佳選擇。

⑪ pressure：壓力

Lagging behind in sales performance, Susan is facing tremendous pressure from her boss.

由於在銷售業績上落後，Susan 正面臨來自她老闆極大的壓力。

⑫ in terms of：就…而言、在…方面

Tim is an excellent sales guy in terms of getting lucrative business.

就拿高利潤訂單這點來說，Tim 是一位極為優秀的業務人員。

⑬ a lot tougher：更困難許多，同**much tougher**

For most salespeople, it is a lot tougher to improve profitability than to increase business volume.

對多數業務人員來說，改善利潤率遠比增加生意量來得困難多了。

⑭ full-capacity：產能滿載的

In the case of full-capacity operations, both planning manager and production manager are under tremendous pressure.

在產能滿載的情況下，生管經理與生產經理二人都面臨非常大的壓力。

⑮ result in：造成、導致

Shortage of inventory results in a great amount of lost business.

庫存不夠導致我們失去好多生意。

⑯ inventory level：庫存水準

Finance department warns us that our inventory level is way too high to accept.

財務部警告我們，庫存水準實在高到無法接受。

⑰ how's everything going?：一切都好嗎？你好嗎？

⑱ how about yourself?：那你自己呢？同問**And you?**

⑲ I need a favor from you.：我需要你幫個忙。

favor 在商場上大多指因為關係好而提供的協助

NOTE

⑳ under your O.A. number MD997：這裡用 "**under**"是指在 **O.A.** 編號 **MD997** 裡的那張訂單

㉑ dig out：挖出、找出
Grace is busy digging out relevant statistics for her boss.
Grace 正忙著找出相關的統計數據給她老闆。

㉒ to pull in by one week：提前一週出貨
Please try your best to pull in by one week.
請盡你所能地提前一週出貨。

㉓ urgently：緊急地、急迫地
Andy urgently called the customer to see why they canceled the order.
Andy 緊急打電話給客戶去了解他們取消訂單的原因。

㉔ original：原始的、原本的、最初的
The revised price our supplier quoted to us is 20% lower than the original one.
我們供應廠商修改過後的報價比原來的便宜了 20%。

㉕ tough：困難、辛苦
常說的運氣不佳可用 bad luck，但 tough luck 更貼切
It is always a tough job for a salesperson to develop new business or new customers.
對業務人員來說，開發新生意或新客戶永遠是一項苦差事。

㉖ at the moment：現在、目前、此時此刻

At the moment, we haven't decided if we're going to fight back.

目前我們還沒決定是否要還擊。

㉗ running at full capacity：在產能滿載的營運狀態

Because of the strong market demand, we are currently running at full capacity.

由於市場需求強勁，我們目前產能滿載。

㉘ doubt：懷疑

Under such circumstances, I doubt we'll be able to match the competitor's price.

在這情況下，我懷疑我們有辦法跟進競爭對手的價格。

㉙ shaky position：很糟糕的情況

We'll be in a shaky position if we lose this loyal account.

若失去這家忠實客戶，我們的處境就很糟糕了。

㉚ fail to meet our customer's request：無法滿足客戶需求

We'll definitely be in deep trouble if we fail to meet our customer's request for better customer service.

如果無法滿足客戶需求提供更好的客戶服務，我們必定會有大麻煩。

NOTE

㉛ very much appreciate：非常感謝

I would very much appreciate your help in solving this application problem.

我非常感謝你協助我們解決這應用上的問題。

㉜ in this regard：在這方面

Thank you so much for being so supportive in this regard.

非常感謝你在這方面如此支持我們。

㉝ lengthy：冗長的、時間拉得很長的

相反的，「簡短的」就用 brief 或 short

I just finished a lengthy conversation with one of our major suppliers concerning possible material shortage in Q3.

我剛剛才結束與一家主要供應商關於第三季可能缺料的冗長對話。

㉞ look for：尋找、期待

Awesome! This solution is exactly what we're looking for.

太讚了！這解決方案正是我們所期待的。

㉟ the day after tomorrow：後天

「前天」是 the day before yesterday

It's late and some of you are on the road tomorrow. We'll have the con-call the day after tomorrow.

現在時間不早了，而你們有幾位明天出差，我們後天視訊會議再談。

36 remaining：其餘的、剩餘的

Please ship whatever you have from stock to us today and the remaining by courier whenever they are ready.

請你們今天把手上所有庫存出給我們，其餘的一旦好了就用快遞寄。

37 according to：根據、依據

I'm afraid we're going to miss the sales target by the end of the year according to the updated Y-T-D data.

根據最新的 Y-T-D 數據來看，到年底恐怕我們將無法達成業務目標。

Y-T-D 是 Year-To-Date 縮寫，表示今年到現今。

38 the best you can do：（你們）已盡全力了

We are not complaining as we know this is the best you can do.

我們沒抱怨，因為我們了解你們已盡全力了。

39 isn't it?：不是這樣嗎？句尾反問，口語常用

Your sales target is reasonable, isn't it?

你的銷售目標很合理，不是嗎？

40 switch：調換、切換、轉換

Switching works to accommodate an urgent request on a CNC machine can be very costly.

為了滿足緊急需求而切換 CNC 加工機的工作，代價會很高。

NOTE

41 abruptly：突然的、無預期的，也可說**suddenly**或**unexpectedly**

42 in such a case：在這情況下

In such a case, we will have a much healthier financial status.

在這情況下，我們的財務狀況會變得更健康。

43 be able to：能夠，也可用**can**、**could**

We'll be able to provide you with online applications service, apart from field application support.

我們除了提供現場應用技術支援之外，也能夠提供你們線上應用服務。

44 sounds good：聽起來不錯、感覺不錯

Danny, are you saying Ace is going to visit us next week? It sounds good.

Danny，你是說 Ace 下星期要來公司拜訪？聽起來真不錯。

45 revised：修改過的

Justine, would you please discard the O.A. that I sent you this morning? I'll send you the revised one in a minute.

Justine，請你將今天上午我傳給你的那張 O.A. 作廢好嗎？我馬上會傳更正版給你。

46 right away：立刻、馬上

Yes Phil, we'll ship it to you from our stock right away.

是的 Phil，我們會立即從庫存裡出貨給你。

47 supportive：樂於幫忙、協助的

Being supportive is imperative for a salesperson.

業務人員必需要有樂於助人的特質。

48 work out well：進行順利，有好結局

After working together for 10 full days, I'm very happy to see things work out well.

在聯手共事 10 天後，很高興看到努力有了好結果。

Lesson 5 下單 – 付款
P.O.：O.A. & Payment

文重點① **Summary 1**

Once the supplier receives the purchase order, it will carefully review several important sections such as "Descriptions", "Unit Price", "Quantity", "Amount", "Delivery", and "Payment". From time to time, problems can arise while dealing with a new customer for the first time, because different companies run different rules. In the following case, the supplier acted in a tough way, insisting that the customer accept the supplier's terms. In practice, as the seller-buyer relationships develop, most suppliers would review the key terms so that the customer can achieve comfort with the deal.

一旦收到客戶訂單，供應商會仔細檢視訂單上的重要項目，內容包括貨品說明、數量、單價、總金額、交期和付款方式。新客戶首次交易，往往因為雙方各有立場而引發爭議。雖然在某些狀況下廠商會採取較強硬作法，讓客戶接受其付款方式。實際上，隨著生意進展，雙方關係亦隨著升溫，多數供應廠商會適時調整付款方式，讓客戶也因信用度提高而得到對等回報而覺得寬心。

下單－付款條件　P.O.：Payment Terms　 5-1

> **Purchaser, Adventure Computer (Singapore)** 採購
> Sam
>
> **Sales Rep, Umax Inc. (Taiwan)** 業務代表
> Christine

Sam: Hi Christine, this is Sam Martin from Adventure Computer. How are you doing today?

嗨 Christine，我是 Adventure Computer 的 Sam Martin。妳今天好嗎？

Christine: Very good, Sam, thanks. I received the purchase order you sent yesterday. Everything is fine except the payment terms.

我很好，謝謝 Sam。我收到你昨天傳來的訂單了。除了付款條件外，其他都沒問題。

Sam: What's wrong with it? We always pay net 60.

付款條件有什麼問題？我們一向都是出貨後 60 天內付清。

Christine: I'm afraid it's not going to work with our company. We can only do business on cash up front with a new dealer like you.

可是我們公司不接受那樣。對於貴公司這類新客戶，我們的原則一向是款到出貨。

Sam: Cash up front? It is not reasonable to a channel partner.

得付現喔？這對我們這種通路夥伴不合理啊！

Christine: I fully understand your point, but it is our long-time policy.

我完全能理解你的感受，不過這是我們公司一向的政策。

: You are <u>tough</u>. When will you start to review the payment terms?

你們真的很嚴格。那你們何時才會考慮變更付款條件呢？

Sam

: We are reviewing it at the end of the year.

我們每年年終會檢討一次。

Christine

: OK then, please send the <u>O.A.</u> to us as soon as possible.

好吧，請妳儘快傳 O.A. 給我。

Sam

: I will. Thanks again for your business.

我會的。再次感謝你的訂單。

Christine

NOTE

① section：部分、區段

Both RFQ and RFP contain several critical sections to which salespeople have to pay more attention.

RFQ 與 RFP 二者都包括幾個關鍵部分，業務人員得特別留意才行。

RFQ 為 Request for Quotation 的縮寫；RFP 則為 Request for Proposal 的縮寫

② from time to time：不時、有時

From time to time, they made mistakes in shipping.

他們不時會在出貨時出錯。

③ arise：出現、發生

You need to stay more focused, otherwise serious problems could arise.

你得更專注些，否則會發生嚴重問題。

NOTE

④ deal with：處理、應付

deal with a new customer 是指和新客戶往來、打交道

⑤ for the first time：第一次、頭一次

We have to be very careful while dealing with an RFQ from this company for the first time.

首次處理這家公司的 RFQ 時我們得特別小心。

⑥ act in a tough way：強硬作為

We acted in a tough way to reject their unreasonable request.

我們強悍拒絕他們無理的要求。

⑦ insist：堅持

insist 後的子句要用原形動詞

The customer is insisting that we maintain our original selling price for this order even though we sent our GRI notice to them two weeks ago.

雖然兩星期前我們已經通知他們全面漲價了，這家客戶仍堅持我們得照舊價格來處理這張訂單。

GRI 是 General Rate Increase 全面漲價的縮寫。

⑧ achieve comfort with：對…感覺受到回報、對…感覺釋懷

Mike was depressed because he hadn't done well on the exam. The advice given by Mrs. Lee allowed him to achieve comfort with the situation.

Mike 為了沒考好而沮喪。聽完李老師的開導，Mike 對於不理想的分數感到釋懷了。

⑨ How are you doing today?：你今天好嗎？

同 How's it going? 或 How are you?

⑩ purchase order：採購訂單、訂單

⑪ except：除了…之外

They are able to meet all of our requirements except the price.

除了價格之外，他們能滿足我們所有的需求。

⑫ payment terms：付款條件

⑬ what's wrong with it?：那有什麼不對嗎？

⑭ net 60：出貨**60**天（現金）付清

According to our agreement, you will be on net 60 for the first 12 months.

根據我們的協議，最初 12 個月的付款期是出貨後 60 天內付清。

⑮ it's not going to work：行不通

The way you service the customer is wrong. It's not going to work.

你服務客戶的方法不對，那樣子是行不通的。

⑯ cash up front：（現金）款到出貨

I believe cash up front is safer for us because this is the first time we received an order from them.

我認為款到出貨對我們比較安全，因為這是我們頭一次接到他們的訂單。

NOTE

⑰ **dealer**：經銷商

Most of the time, dealers care more about their margin than anything else.

多數時候，經銷商在意他們本身的利潤遠勝於其他任何因素。

⑱ **channel partner**：通路夥伴，多指代理商或經銷商

They have been one of our most reliable channel partners for more than twenty years.

二十多年以來，他們一直都是我們最可靠的通路夥伴之一。

⑲ **long-time policy**：長久的政策

It has been our long-time policy to do strict credit checks on each and every new customer.

對每個新客戶實施嚴格的信用查核是我們長久以來的政策。

⑳ **tough**：嚴格、強悍、難搞

Our finance department is always playing tough when dealing with late payment.

我們財務部在處理延遲付款時總是很強悍。

㉑ **O. A.**：訂單確認，**Order Acknowledgment** 的縮寫

文重點② Summary 2

Supplier's payment terms do not change without a sound reason. Most suppliers are conservative while reviewing requests from customers to change payment terms. A credit check on the customer is always essential under any circumstances. If properly executed, it will provide the suppliers with sufficient security in payment collection. Furthermore, in a case of revising payment terms for the customer, credit check would serve as an evaluation base on which the final decision is made.

若非有充分的理由，供應廠商的付款條件是不太會變的。一旦現有客戶提出更改付款條件要求，廠商也多半會極為保守地謹慎行事。新通路夥伴在經過一段期間以現金方式交易後，多半會向供應商提出要求，改為較為優惠的付款方式，如記帳。供應廠商會在接獲要求後，進行客戶信用查核。經由銀行體系或專業信用調查機構，確認客戶支付能力與信用紀錄，做為調整付款方式的重要依據。

信用查核　Credit Check 5-2

> **Sam** 😊：**Purchaser, Adventure Computer (Singapore)** 採購
>
> **Christine** 😊：**Sales Rep, Umax Inc. (Taiwan)** 業務代表

😊 **Sam**：Good afternoon, Christine, this is Sam Martin from Adventure Computer, how are you doing today?

Christine，下午好，我是 Adventure Computer 的 Sam Martin。妳今天好嗎？

😊 **Christine**：Good afternoon, Sam. I'm doing fine, thanks. How about yourself?

午安，Sam。我很好，謝謝。那你呢？

😊 **Sam**：Pretty good. I'm calling to discuss with you about revising your payment terms that I mentioned to you last week.

還不錯。打電話給妳，是想和妳討論上星期我提的修改付款條件的事。

Dr. Lee 解析

> 直接說明來電目的，就是想討論有關變更付款條件事宜。

😊 **Christine**：I'm glad that you called. I'm holding a 2-page application form that must be filled out by you before we proceed. I'll send it to you in a minute.

很高興你來電。我現在手上有一份兩頁的申請書,得讓你填寫完成才能去申請,我等一下傳給你。

Dr. Lee 解析

制度健全的廠商多備有變更付款條件的申請表格,讓客戶填寫相關資訊。一份二頁的申請表格其實還不算要求太多,外商上市公司通常都會要求更多資料。

☺ : What? A 2-page application form? My goodness! How much
Sam   stuff should we fill out?

什麼呀!兩頁的申請表格喔?我的老天,到底要我們填多少資料啊?

Dr. Lee 解析

通常客戶都會表示還要填一堆資料實在不可思議。

☺ : Actually, it's not too bad. What our finance department
Christine   requested is only basic business information and certain key
    financial information.

沒那麼糟糕啦!我們財務部要的資料,都只是公司基本資料和一些關鍵財務資料而已。

Dr. Lee 解析

> 要求的資料，一部分屬於公司基本資料，另一部分則是公司財務資料。

☺ ： Let me tell you, this is sensitive information. I had a very
Sam unpleasant experience a few months back asking our finance
department for some bank information. And now you are giving
me a hard time again.

妳聽我說，那些都是敏感資料。幾個月前，我要求財務部門提供一些銀行資料，那次經驗真是不愉快。現在妳又給我這難題。

Dr. Lee 解析

> 站在客戶立場，會對廠商要求提供這類敏感資訊感到困擾與擔心。本身內部溝通起來，往往也是困難重重。因此，客戶才會對廠商抱怨這是在找麻煩。

☺ ： I fully understand your position, but please do try hard to
Christine supply us with sufficient information as it is the only way to
get approved. Please do help me to help you in this regard.

我完全理解你的立場，不過真的要請你多幫忙，儘可能提供足夠資訊給我們，因為那是唯一能夠讓你們過關的方法。請你務必在這方面多幫忙。

Dr. Lee 解析

在買賣雙方各有立場的情況下，最佳解決方式就是協商。看在長遠生意配合份上，在此客戶雖然口頭小抱怨，還是會設法配合，畢竟付款方式對於新進通路夥伴非常重要。

Sam：OK. I'll see what exactly are requested and touch base with our finance manager.

好的。我會去了解到底得提供哪些資料，再來設法和財務經理溝通。

Dr. Lee 解析

雖然覺得麻煩，但為了自身利益著想，客戶還是得想辦法配合。

Christine：Thanks. I'm very sorry for all the cumbersome procedure, but I know you'll be able to work it out.

謝謝。那些手續很繁瑣，真不好意思。不過我知道你有辦法搞定的。

Dr. Lee 解析

場面話會讓對方好受些。

☺ Sam : I really hope so. What will be the new payment term if we are approved?

真希望如此啊！如果我們申請過關了，那新的付款條件會是怎樣？

Dr. Lee 解析

再確認新付款方式內容。

☺ Christine : I was <u>proposing</u> net 60 to meet your original request. And I think you <u>deserve</u> it, <u>judging from</u> the <u>contribution</u> your company made to us in the last six months.

我是替你們爭取 60 天付款，來滿足你們原來的要求。從過去半年你們對我們公司的貢獻來看，我認為那是你們應得的待遇。

Dr. Lee 解析

客戶對廠商的貢獻度扮演重要角色。貢獻度越高，通過審核的機率也高。

☺ Sam : OK, I'll check the form out <u>real quick</u> and hopefully come back to you <u>in a day or two</u>. How long will it take to get approved?

好的，我會快快檢查一下申請表格，希望能在一、兩天之內回覆妳。通常得花多久時間才能通過審核？

Dr. Lee 解析

了解審核作業要多久。

Christine：<u>In general</u>, it takes one full week for us to approve. If you need anything from me, <u>please feel free to call</u>.
一般來說，我們需要一星期的作業時間，有問題儘管打電話給我。

Dr. Lee 解析

需要花多少時間的動詞最常用「take」。這裡需要一星期跑流程，就說「it takes one full week ...」

Sam：I will. Thanks a lot.
我會的，多謝妳。

Christine：No problem. I really want <u>to get it done</u> quicker.
不客氣，我真想快一點把這件事搞定。

Dr. Lee 解析

「get it done」是說完成某件事或搞定某個問題。在口語常用這種被動式說法。

NOTE

❶ sound：有充分理由的

He gave us a sound explanation for the delay in shipping last week.

對於上週延遲出貨，他做了合理的解釋。

❷ credit check：徵信、信用調查

Most of the time, we do credit check through banks.

我們多半透過銀行進行徵信。

❸ essential：必要的、不可少的

It is absolutely essential to collect money in full on time.

我們絕對要準時收到全數貨款。

❹ under any circumstances：無論如何、在任何情況下

You have to hand in the report by 5 p.m. today under any circumstances.

無論如何，你得在今天下午 5 點前交出報告。

❺ if properly executed：如果執行恰當的話

If properly executed, I'm confident that the GRI will succeed in the end.

如果執行恰當的話，我有信心 GRI 終將成功。

GRI 是 General Rate Increase（全面漲價）的縮寫

NOTE

6 sufficient：足夠的、充分的

We have sufficient evidence that TXC undercut us by 60 cents and got the order.

我們握有充分證據，TXC 以一個比我們低 6 角錢的價格拿到訂單。

7 collection：收取、收集，商業上是指收款

Payment collection is one of the most important responsibilities of a salesperson.

收款是業務人員最重要的責任之一。

8 furthermore：此外、而且

Furthermore, we provide our customers with online technical service.

此外，我們還提供客戶線上技術服務。

9 serve as：當作、作為

The email serves as a formal notice of the GRI which will become effective on July 1.

這封電郵作為即將在 7 月 1 日起生效之 GRI 的正式通知。

10 evaluation base：考核基準

Collection performance becomes an important part of the evaluation base for a salesperson.

收款績效成為業務人員考核基準中很重要的一部分。

NOTE

⑪ **I'm doing fine**：我很好，也可簡單說 **I'm fine.** 或只說 **Fine.**

⑫ **pretty good**：很好、很不錯，口語常用

⑬ **I'm glad that you called**：我很高興你來電

⑭ **in a minute**：很快，不代表就是一分鐘，通常會稍久些

I'll call you back in a minute.
我會很快回你電話。

⑮ **a 2-page application form**：一份二頁的申請表格

這裡二頁的寫法 2-page 是形容詞，而不是 2 pages

⑯ **my goodness**：天啊、我的老天啊！

驚嘆語，不建議用 Oh my God

My goodness! We won the bid!
天啊！我們拿到標案了！

⑰ **fill out**：填寫、填滿

Would you please fill these forms out before I tell you how to proceed?
能請你先填好這些表格，我再告訴你如何進行好嗎？

⑱ key：重要的

Excellent technical support has been one of the key competitive edges we possessed.

優質的技術支援一直是我們擁有的一項重要競爭優勢。

⑲ let me tell you：我告訴你

這是一種口氣比較直接的說法，也可說 Please note

Let me tell you, the best way to win their business is to help them solve the applications problems with our products.

我來告訴你，贏得他們生意最好的辦法，就是用我們的產品幫他們解決應用上的問題。

⑳ sensitive：敏感的

I will call a management meeting for the sensitive issues like salary raise and promotion.

我將召集一次主管會議來討論敏感事項，例如加薪和升遷。

㉑ unpleasant：不愉快的

We had an unpleasant experience doing business with Ace Metal a few years ago.

幾年前我們和 Ace Metal 生意往來時，曾經有一段很不愉快的經驗。

㉒ a few months back：幾個月前，同 **a few months ago**，較口語說法

We bought the machine from Pinnacle Machines a few months back.

這臺機器是我們在幾個月前向 Pinnacle Machines 買的。

NOTE

㉓ give me a hard time：讓我不好過、找我麻煩

It took more than 5 hours for me to clear the shipment through customs. I think they were giving me a hard time.

我花了 5 個多小時才辦好這筆貨的通關，我想他們是在找我麻煩。

㉔ get approved：被審核通過

It took us tons of R&D efforts to get approved.

我們在研發上下了好大的工夫才通過認證。

㉕ in this regard：這件事、這方面，也可說 **on this subject**

I must say you're right in this regard.

我必須說在這方面你是對的。

㉖ cumbersome procedure：煩人的手續、麻煩的程序

Please bear with such cumbersome procedures.

手續很繁雜，還請你多多包涵。

㉗ work it out：解決

I'm not worrying at all. I believe you'll be able to work it out.

我一點都不擔心，我相信你有辦法解決的。

NOTE

㉘ propose：提議、建議

Eddie was proposing to delay the meeting when we were told that Susan had been stuck on the highway.

當我們得知 Susan 困在高速公路上時，Eddie 正提議將會議延後舉行。

㉙ deserve：應得

Their design deserves the prize as the design team has been working so hard in the past 12 months.

他們的設計得獎是應該的，因為設計團隊過去 12 個月來非常辛苦地工作。

㉚ judging from：根據……來判斷

The company seems to be in trouble, judging from the fact that it paid us so late.

從這家公司付款這麼慢來判斷，他們營運似乎有問題。

㉛ contribution：貢獻

Being with the company for more than 20 years, Tom has made an enormous contribution in terms of business development.

Tom 待在公司超過 20 年，在業務開發方面有很大的貢獻。

㉜ real quick：快快地

美式口語較常使用，這裡是指 take a quick look

No problem, Dan. I'll send you our quotation real quick.

沒問題，Dan，我會快快傳報價單給你。

NOTE

㉝ in a day or two：一、二天之內

We'll pay by wire in a day or two.

我們會在一二天之內電匯付款。

㉞ in general：一般來說、大致來說

In general, class-A customers pay us in 60 days.

一般來說，A 級客戶的付款期限是 60 天。

㉟ please feel free to call：請別客氣，儘管打電話給我

If you have any questions, please feel free to call me.

如果你有任何問題，請別客氣，儘管打電話給我。

㊱ to get it done：完成或解決某件事

這裡用被動式表示，口語經常使用

Guys, it's getting dark. Let's get it done now.

喂！大夥兒，天要黑了，我們快點把這完成吧！

Lesson 6 客戶服務：不良品退回
CS：Handling Returns

文重點① Summary 1

In the era of competition as of today, customer service, CS, has become an important competitive advantage for all business entities. It creates added value to the customers in a more economical way. Particularly in B2B mode, customer service forms a reliable and long-term customer value. One of the most-often-seen customer services is return handling. Although the CS module of an ERP system provides a procedural platform for both parties to follow, the physical return handling service provided by the CS staffs is crucial to enhance customer relationships. By effective day-to-day execution, customer service could become an important part of the business culture. By then, such competitive advantage will not be as easily duplicated by the competitors as is the case for pricing or promotion does.

當今企業，無不處心積慮，想在各產業中勝出。除了比成本與獨特性外，客戶服務水平也迅速成為差異化的主角，在企業經營成長策略中的重要性日益升高。

特別是在 B2B 模式裡，企業投資客戶服務的資本支出，比起投資研發、工程、製程或行銷上，相對低很多，卻能夠透過有效的執行，長期下來形成企業文化的一部分，也是一項可靠的客戶價值，更是一項比較不容易模仿複製的競爭策略。退貨處理是最常見的客戶服務項目之一，卻也是客戶日常抱怨的主要來源。近年來，企業資源規劃系統（ERP）多已將退貨處理功能納入行銷或業務模組裡，提供買賣雙方極為便利的操作平臺。不過日常實體客服功能與客服人員所提供的服務品質，依舊是最重要的客戶接觸點，也是客戶滿意度最直接的衝擊力量。

退貨　Returns  6-1

> **Kevin**：**Purchaser, Delta Electronics (Singapore)** 採購
>
> **Lynn**：**Customer Service Specialist, Rock Lake Inc. (Taiwan)** 客服專員

Kevin：Hi, this is Kevin Johnson from Delta Electronics. I'd like to speak to Bob Krall.

嗨，我是 Delta Electronics 的 Kevin Johnson，我找 Bob Krall。

Lynn：Hi Kevin, this is Lynn Stafford. I'm the customer service contact of the sales department. I'm sorry Bob is not available at the moment. How may I help you?

嗨 Kevin，我叫 Lynn Stafford，是業務部客服專員。很抱歉，Bob 不在位置上，我能幫你嗎？

Kevin：Lynn, we have a problem with the recent shipment.

Lynn，我們剛進來的一批貨有些問題。

Lynn：I'm very sorry to hear that. What's the problem?

真是抱歉，是什麼問題？

Kevin：It seemed to me that you sent a wrong shipment to us.

你們似乎出錯貨了。

Lynn：It is a serious mistake and we are very sorry about that. Can you tell me the shipping advice number please?

那可是嚴重疏失，真的非常抱歉。能請你告訴我出貨通知單號嗎？

Kevin：Yeah, it reads RL7703-21005.

可以，RL7703-21005。

Lynn：OK, please send it back to us <u>with the RMA number</u> WS10899. We will <u>investigate</u> the case immediately.

好，請你將那批貨退回給我們，並註明 RMA 號 WS10899，我們會立刻調查這件事。

Kevin：So the RMA number is WS10899. OK, we'll send it back to you later. <u>How about</u> our shipment?

那我重複一次，RMA 號 WS10899。好，我稍後就會退回，但我們那批貨呢？

Lynn：Actually I'm <u>checking with</u> our shipping guy now. Oh, your shipment is still in our warehouse. We will ship to you right away.

我正在和出貨人員核對中。喔！那批貨還在庫房裡，我們馬上就出貨給你。

Kevin：Great, thanks very much.

那太好了，謝謝你。

Lynn：Not a problem, that's what we should have done right <u>in the beginning</u>. We are very sorry to <u>have caused you trouble</u>.

哪裡，我們一開始就該做好的，非常抱歉造成你們困擾。

NOTE

1 era：年代、時代

We are in an era of virtual everything in which business is being done without human involvement.

我們正處於一個不需人類參與就能成交生意的全虛擬時代。

2 as of today：到今天

As of today, Bruce has been the Ace in our team.

直到今天，Bruce 都是我們團隊中的王牌。

3 customer service：客戶服務

Good customer service quality differentiates ourselves from all others.

良好的客戶服務品質讓我們與眾不同。

4 competitive advantage：競爭優勢

Flexible pricing is one of our competitive advantages.

彈性定價策略是我們諸多競爭優勢之一。

5 business entity：企業體

B2B or B2B2C, sales is always the most important function in a private business entity.

無論 B2B 或 B2B2C，業務永遠是私人企業體最重要的企業功能。

NOTE

⑥ **added value**：增值、附加價值

Quality customer service is an added value most often perceived by the customer.

最常讓客戶感受到的附加價值就是高品質的客戶服務。

⑦ **economical**：經濟的、划算的、節省的

Conference call or video conference is a lot more economical than a physical meeting.

多方電話會議或視訊會議要比實體會議來得划算許多。

⑧ **B2B mode**：B2B 模式

In a B2B mode, customer relationship means everything to the salespeople.

在 B2B 模式裡，客戶關係是業務人員的一切。

⑨ **form**：形成、構成

Our excellent online customer service and applications service form a solid company asset.

我們超人一等的線上客戶服務和應用服務，建構了公司的堅實資產。

⑩ **reliable**：可靠的、可信賴的

Frequency Technology is famous for providing reliable crystal oscillators at a reasonable price level.

Frequency Technology 是以供應合理價位、品質可靠的石英震盪器聞名。

NOTE

⑪ customer value：客戶價值

In order to enhance the overall customer value, we invest heavily in applications support and online customer service.

為了強化整體客戶價值，我們大量投資在應用支援和線上客戶服務上。

⑫ most-often-seen：最常見到的

Price cutting is the most-often-seen competition tactic in a matured industry.

在一個飽和產業裡，降價是最常見的一種競爭手段。

⑬ return handling：退貨處理

Fred has been busy with a number of tough return handling issues since he stepped into the office this morning.

Fred 從早上進辦公室後，就一直忙著處理好幾項難搞的退貨案件。

⑭ module：模組、模塊

Most ERP systems are composed of different modules such as BOM module, MRP module, Cost module, Sales module, and many others.

大多數 ERP 系統是由不同功能模塊組成，如 BOM 模組、MRP 模組、Cost 模組、Sales 模組、以及其它很多模組。

⑮ ERP system：企業資源規劃系統

A well designed ERP system will help employee improve work efficiency.

一個設計周全的 ERP 系統能幫助員工改善工作效率。

NOTE

⑯ **procedural platform**：程序平臺

The customer service module provides both the customer and the manufacturer a convenient procedural platform to interact with each other.

客戶服務模塊提供買賣雙方便利的互動程序平臺。

⑰ **both parties**：客戶和製造廠、買賣雙方

⑱ **physical**：實體、實際

Nowadays online customer service facilitates sellers and buyers to interact without a physical face to face meeting.

現今線上客服功能讓買賣雙方不需實際會面就能有效互動。

⑲ **crucial to**：重要

Being responsive is crucial to handling returns.

快速回應對於退貨處理非常重要。

⑳ **enhance**：加強、強化

As a result of the recent return incident, we were requested to enhance the emotion management of our customer service staff.

由於近期一次退貨事件，上級要求我們加強客服人員情緒管理。

21 customer relationships：客戶關係

Speaking of customer relationships, Loraine always receives high regards from her boss.

說起客戶關係，Loraine 總是得到他老闆的高度讚賞。

22 day-to-day：日常的、每日的

I'm randomly watching the day-to-day activities of my salespeople through CRM.

我藉由 CRM 隨機觀察業務人員每天的活動。

23 execution：執行

To get better result from the CRM system, effective execution by the salespeople is the key.

CRM 要有好結果，業務人員的有效執行是一大關鍵。

24 business culture：企業文化

Being a team player has become an important part of our business culture.

打團體戰已經成為我們企業文化中很重要的一部分。

25 by then：到那時

Take it easy, Nancy. If you hang in there for two more weeks, you'll make it by then.

Nancy，別緊張。只要再堅持二星期，到時候妳就會成功的。

NOTE

㉖ **duplicate**：複製

Mark, I'd insist that you stop undercutting our competitors as it's so easy to duplicate.

Mark，我很堅持你不要再殺價競爭了，因為這伎倆太容易複製。

㉗ **as is the case for pricing or promotion**：
如同定價與促銷那樣，可以被競爭者複製

這表示先前說的 "customer service" 若已經成為公司文化，競爭對手想複製就不是像降價或是促銷那麼容易

Tony, please reconsider raising your quote to Suntek, as Frank did with Central Steel.

Tony，請你考慮比照 Frank 調高對 Central Steel 的價格，也提高你對 Suntek 的報價。

㉘ **is not available**：指不在辦公室內或座位上，而無法親自接聽電話

Wendy, if Oscar is not available, who should I speak to regarding pricing?

Wendy，如果 Oscar 現在不方便說話，我該找誰談價格呢？

㉙ **at the moment**：當下、現在

Shelly, nothing we can do at the moment except wait and see.

Shelly，現在我們啥也不能做，只能靜觀其變。

㉚ how may I help you?：我能幫你什麼忙嗎？

是一句很有禮貌的常用對話，也能說 How can I help you? 或 What can I do for you?

㉛ have a problem with：有問題

這裡 problem 後介系詞用 with，表示問題的指向性，指的是最近的進貨

Jessy, I do have a problem with the drawings you sent to me the other day.

Jessy，我對於你昨天下午傳給我的圖紙有疑問。

㉜ it seemed to me：對我來說似乎……

也可直接用 It seemed 省略 to me

It seemed we had a serious problem with our testing instruments.

我們測試儀器的問題似乎很嚴重。

㉝ shipping advice number：出貨通知編號

Bonnie, please tell me the shipping advice number for the shipment we just released to Baxton Paper.

Bonnie，請告訴我剛剛出給 Baxton Paper 那筆貨的出貨通知號碼。

NOTE

㉞ with the RMA number：連同 RMA 號碼一起

RMA 是 Return Merchandise Authorization（退貨授權或退貨許可）的縮寫

Dennis, you need to get an RMA number from the manufacturer before you start the return procedure.

Dennis，在你啓動退貨程序之前，得先從廠商那裡拿到 RMA 號碼。

㉟ investigate：調查

Ruby, Please give us a few days to investigate the case.

Ruby，請給我們幾天時間調查這案件。

㊱ how about：如何？怎麼樣？

How about I go visit you on Wednesday?

我星期三去拜訪你如何？

㊲ check with：和…核對

Sandy, I'll check with our QA guy first and get back to you ASAP.

Sandy，我先和 QA 人員核對一下再儘快回覆妳。

㊳ in the beginning：剛開始、起初

Rex, regarding the defectives, you should have told me in the beginning.

Rex，關於那些不良品，你一開始就該告訴我。

39 have caused you trouble：引起麻煩

這裡用現在完成式，強調已經發生

Mr. Robinson, please accept my apology as I realize the incidents have caused you lots of trouble.

Robinson 先生，請接受我的道歉。我知道這些事件已經帶給你們極大的麻煩。

課文重點② Summary 2

The 8D-Report is actually part of the "Eight Disciplines Problem Solving (8D)" program and has widely been used by <u>an increasing number</u> of manufacturers, particularly the electronics <u>firms</u>, as a standard <u>corrective</u> operation. When a <u>customer complaint</u> <u>arises</u>, it will be much better if the complaint is to be handled in a <u>systematic way</u> so that the customer <u>is</u> closely <u>kept in the loop</u> and <u>timely</u> <u>informed of</u> the progress made for the complaint. The <u>core concept</u> of 8D program is to timely detect, <u>verify</u>, and <u>resolve</u> the problems that were reported to the company <u>through whatever the channel</u>. The <u>mechanism</u> is to <u>identify</u>, correct and <u>eliminate</u> <u>recurring problems</u> so that the customer understands not only why the problems occurred but also how they are resolved and avoided in the future. Most importantly, the problems are <u>permanently</u> corrected and won't happen again in the future. In the end, the customer will receive a copy of 8D-Report in which all the <u>disciplines</u> are <u>well documented</u>.

An 8D report will include a starting section of <u>general problem description</u> and then followed by D1: Team members, the team; D2: Description of problem; D3:

Interim containment actions; D4: Define the root cause; D5: Choose and verify permanent corrective actions; D6: Validate permanent corrective actions; D7: Prevent recurrence of the problem; and D8: Congratulate the team.

Remark：It has become a trend that a D0 be added with an overall plan to solve the problem.

在當今製造業，尤其是電子相關產業裡，客訴處理不當，往往會造成嚴重後果，包括可能的龐大違約賠償金額。因此，多數具規模電子廠商的品保部門，都採用 8D 問題解決模式，以結構性、系統性的方式，來處理各種形式的客訴。這 8D 的核心概念，就是將經由各種管道反饋回企業內部的客訴，進行及時的問題偵測、查證並解決。而 8D 的實際運作機制，就是確認問題點，加以改正，並徹底排除重複發生的可能性。另外，透過 8D 書面報告，讓客戶清楚了解問題發生的根本原因，以及問題排除改正的方法，並保證不再重複發生。所有 8D 的重要詳細資訊，均記載於 8D 報告內。

一份 8D 報告內容，由問題綜述開始後，就包括D1 到 D8 如下：D1：成立問題解決團隊；D2：敘述問題：D3：臨時措施內容；D4：界定問題根本原因；D5：決定並求證永久改正措施；D6：驗證永久改正措施；D7：防止問題重複發生；D8：替團隊成員打氣。附註：近幾年的趨勢是多加D0：解決問題的整體計畫。

改正 – 8D 報告　Correction：8D Report 6-2

Kevin ： **Purchaser, Delta Electronics (Singapore)** 採購

Bob ： **Deputy Sales Manager, Rock Lake Inc. (Taiwan)**
業務副理

Kevin ： Hey Bob, this is Kevin Johnson from Delta Electronics. How are you doing today?

嘿 Bob，我是 Delta Eletronics 的 Kevin Johnson，你今天好嗎？

最常用的問候句。

Bob ： Good afternoon, Kevin. I'm doing fine, thanks. How about yourself?

Kevin，午安。我很好，謝謝。你呢？

最常用的問候句回覆。

Kevin : Very good. I'm calling to tell you that my boss asked me to <u>hold a meeting</u> next Monday to review the <u>incident</u>, <u>I mean</u> the <u>wrong shipment you made to us</u> a couple of days ago. Although it was <u>delayed by two days only</u>, it caused serious trouble to our <u>production line</u>.

我很好。打電話來是要告訴你，我老闆要我下週一主持一次檢討會，檢討兩天前貴公司出錯貨的事件。雖然那只延誤了二天，卻嚴重打亂了我們的生產線。

Dr. Lee 解析

由於該次事件影響到生產，客戶採購 Kevin 奉上司指示，得主持檢討會。因此，Kevin 急於要求供應廠商業務 Bob 儘速提供相關資訊。

Bob : Yeah, Lynn told me about it after I <u>returned from</u> my trip yesterday. I'm very sorry it caused so much trouble to you. <u>In fact</u>, I was planning to talk with our QA people regarding this case later today.

是的。昨天我出差回來，Lynn 就告訴我了。這失誤帶給你們這麼大的麻煩，我感到很抱歉。事實上，我正準備在今天稍晚要和我們品保部門討論這件事。

Dr. Lee 解析

身為業務人員，千萬不要忘記再次道歉。至此，Bob 已經在安排與品保單位討論這個案了。

Kevin : <u>It sounds good to me</u>, but would you please send me a report explaining why the wrong shipment was made and how such a mistake will be avoided in the future.

聽你這樣說挺好的,不過能不能請你準備一份報告給我,說明出錯貨的原因,以及未來你們如何防止這種錯誤再次發生。

Dr. Lee 解析

有些等不及,此時採購 Kevin 還是急於了解出錯貨的原因,以及未來供應商要如何防止錯誤再發生。這也是檢討會的唯一議題。

Bob : I will surely do this as quickly as I can. Basically, our QA people will set up an 8D project particularly for this case. <u>In the end</u>, we will <u>come up with</u> an 8D report <u>covering</u> all the <u>relevant</u> information you may want to know. Once the 8D report is <u>available</u>, I'll send it to you right away.

我一定會儘早準備給你的。基本上,我們品保人員會為這事件成立專案。到頭來,會出一份 8D 報告給你們,裡面有一切你想要了解的相關資訊。一旦 8D 報告出來,我立刻會傳一份給你的。

Dr. Lee 解析

業務 Bob 先以口頭說明處理方式,讓 Kevin 能有個初步理解。

Kevin: An 8D report? What's that? Please don't send anything I'll have difficulties to understand. It <u>has been</u> a <u>nightmare</u> to me <u>already</u>.

一份 8D 報告？那是啥？可別傳給我看不懂的東西好嗎？這事件對我來說已經是場噩夢了。

Dr. Lee 解析

顯然採購 Kevin 壓力有增無減，現在又跑出沒見過的 8D 報告，焦慮心情清楚可見。

Bob: I understand and please relax a little bit. I'm going to give you a <u>brief introduction</u> of the 8D program that we <u>put into force</u> <u>within</u> our company. It <u>serves to</u> resolve all kinds of problems we face <u>on a daily basis</u>. And of course, I'll tell you what an 8D report is.

我懂，請你放輕鬆點。我會向你扼要說明這套用來解決日常發生問題的 8D 方案。當然，我也會告訴你什麼是 8D 報告。

Dr. Lee 解析

對許多產業來說，雖然處理客訴的方式和內涵與 8D 方案相類似，不過就是欠缺制度化管理與運作，無法有效累積知識與經驗。因此，對於初接觸 8D 的客戶，確實需要多加解釋。

Kevin : That's great. Please go ahead and I'll interrupt whenever I'm not following you, OK?

太好了。這就請你說明嘍！如果我中間有聽不懂的地方，我會打斷發問的。好嗎？

Dr. Lee 解析

至此，採購 Kevin 總算能稍微安心了。

Bob : Yes, please. I'll start with the 8D program. Actually it is part of our QA system. It is being implemented company-wide by us as a systematic way of solving problems of all kinds.

好，沒問題。我就從 8D 方案開始。實際上，8D 方案屬於公司品保制度的一部分，也是公司各部門用來制度化解決各類問題的方法。

Dr. Lee 解析

當今的業務必須是通才，對於公司的品保制度，一定得有充分了解才行。這裡可看出，8D 其實是品保的重要項目之一。

Kevin : Excuse me, Bob. Does 8D stand for something?

對不起，Bob。這 8D 是代表什麼嗎？

Dr. Lee 解析

這是業務最常被問到的問題之一。

☺ ： Yes Kevin. It stands for 8 disciplines. Actually, the full
Bob   program name is the "Eight Disciplines Problem Solving".
       You can easily <u>tell from</u> the full name that it is a <u>problem
       solving system</u>.

       是的，Kevin。8D 代表 8 項紀律或規範，實際上 8D 方案全名
       是「Eight Disciplines Problem Solving」，你很容易就能從全
       名看出，這是一種解決問題的制度。

Dr. Lee 解析

8D 的定義與定位很清楚，就是一種系統化解決問題的制度。

☺ ： I see. It sounds complicated, doesn't it?
Kevin 原來如此。聽起來滿複雜的，不是嗎？

☺ ： Not at all. I'm not <u>going into details</u> as it will be <u>a lot easier</u>
Bob   just to review the 8D report. Basically, the report covers all
       you need to know. However, I'd like to <u>focus on</u> the <u>core
       concept</u> of 8D. <u>In brief</u>, it is to detect, verify, and resolve the
       problem and to make sure that the same problem won't happen
       again.

       一點都不複雜。我不會講細節，因為直接來看 8D 報告是最容
       易理解的。基本上，8D 報告能提供所有你想知道的資訊。不

過，我還是想聚焦在 8D 的核心概念。說簡短些，那就是及時發覺、查證、解決問題，並確保相同問題不再發生。

Dr. Lee 解析

直接拿 8D 報告來說明，其實是一種最有效的理解方式。8D 其實是圍繞著「發覺、查證、解決與確保」的核心概念在運作。

Kevin : Very good. I'll further review the 8D report real quick. Thanks very much.

太好了，我會快快去檢視這份 8D 報告的。多謝了。

Dr. Lee 解析

只要了解 8D 核心概念，其餘就去檢視 8D 報告內容行了。

Bob : My pleasure. I do believe you'll see how serious we are in dealing with the problems that we caused.

那是我的榮幸。我相信你會了解，我們是多麼認真處理問題的。

Dr. Lee 解析

這樣制度化的品保做法，確實會讓客戶感到比較安心。

NOTE

❶ an increasing number：愈來愈多的、不斷增加的

An increasing number of international couriers offer next-day delivery service.

愈來愈多的國際快遞公司提供次日交貨服務。

❷ firm：廠商、公司行號

There are many firms competing in the system.

在這產業系統裡有很多家廠商在競爭。

❸ corrective：改正的、矯正的

Albert, we need to work out a corrective action proposal and send it to Benton Steel ASAP.

Albert，我們得儘快提出一份改正方案傳給 Benton Steel。

❹ customer complaint：客戶抱怨、客訴

We're not afraid of receiving customer complaints. We are afraid of not handling them well.

我們不怕收到客戶抱怨，我們只怕沒把客訴處理好。

❺ arise：發生、出現

Cool. If a similar situation arises in the future, we'll have something to refer to.

酷喔！將來如果出現類似情況，我們就有東西可參考了。

NOTE

❻ **systematic way**：有系統的方式、有組織的方式

The con-call this morning went very well in a systematic way.

早上的多方電話會議進行得很有組織且順利。

❼ **keep in the loop**：隨時讓某人或某些人知道重要動態或決定

Don't worry, Sara, I'll keep all of you in the loop.

Sara，別擔心，我會隨時讓你們知道新進展。

❽ **timely**：及時、適時

Fortunately, our engineers resolved electro-mechanical problems of the testing machine in a timely manner.

幸好我們的工程師們及時解決了測試機的機電問題。

❾ **be informed of**：被告知、被通知

All of us were informed of the good news that we won all the three government tenders.

我們都被告知已贏得所有三項政府標案的好消息。

❿ **core concept**：核心概念

The core concept of Post Mortem Documentation (PMD) is to review the successes and failures and document them for future reference.

PMD 的核心概念就是檢討專案成功點與失敗點，並記錄成冊作為未來的參考。

NOTE

⑪ **verify**：證實、驗證

Usually, we ask quality engineers to verify the root cause of a damaged product.

通常我們會請品保工程師來驗證產品損壞的根本原因。

⑫ **resolve**：解決、決心

Our FAEs successfully resolved the mechanical failure caused by thermal expansion.

我們的應用工程師成功解決了因熱脹冷縮導致的機械故障。

⑬ **through whatever the channel**：無論透過哪種管道

We must tackle each and every customer complaint that reached us through whatever the channel.

無論是透過哪種管道收到的客戶抱怨，我們都得逐一解決。

⑭ **mechanism**：機制、運作機制

In the case of returns, the RMA number ignited the entire mechanism of the 8D system.

就退貨來說，RMA 號碼啓動了整個 8D 系統。

⑮ **identify**：辨認、識別

Through online troubleshooting service, we are able to identify many quality problems a lot quicker.

透過線上偵錯服務，我們能夠更快辨認出很多品質問題。

⑯ eliminate：消除、排除

In order to upgrade our service quality, we must eliminate such documentation mistakes.

為了提升服務品質，我們必須根除這種紀錄上的疏失。

⑰ recurring problems：重複發生的問題

Recurring problems will definitely annoy customers.

重複發生問題絕對會激怒客戶的。

⑱ permanently：永久的

After a thorough debugging, we hope our long-time headache will be gone permanently.

在徹底除錯後，希望長期以來讓我們頭痛的問題能永久消失。

⑲ discipline：紀律、訓練、規矩、規定條文

One of the disciplines our sales team sticks with is listening, instead of talking, to the customers more.

我們業務團隊堅持的紀律之一，是多聽客戶說，而不是自己說個不停。

As a sales manager, I pay a lot of attention to disciplines at work.

身為業務經理，我很在意工作紀律。

⑳ well documented：有完整文件紀錄的

All the returns are very well documented by the 8D program in our ERP system.

在我們 ERP 系統裡，所有的退貨案件都在 ERP 8D 程序中留有完整文件紀錄。

NOTE

㉑ **general problem description**：問題綜述
8D 報告的起始章節，8D 報告標題請參考課文重點 2

㉒ **interim**：臨時的、過渡期的（D3）

㉓ **root cause**：根本原因（D4）

㉔ **validate**：驗證（D6）

㉕ **recurrence**：重複發生（D7）

㉖ **congratulate**：打氣、恭賀（D8）

㉗ **overall plan**：整體計畫（D0）

㉘ **hold a meeting**：主持會議

Michelle will hold a meeting this afternoon to announce a new customer service procedure.

Michelle 今天下午將主持一場會議，宣布一套新的客服作業程序。

㉙ **incident**：事件

The quality incident last week didn't do much harm to the relationships between Borden Chemical and us.

上星期的品質事件並沒有影響到我們和 Borden Chemical 之間的關係。

NOTE

㉚ **I mean**：我是說

We have to match TXC's price, Tom. I mean we're going to keep Thompson Metal in our pocket.

Tom，我們得跟進 TXC 的報價，我是說我們要保住 Thompson Metal。

㉛ **wrong shipment you made to us**：出錯貨給我們

出貨在這裡用 shipment made 而不用 shipment shipped

㉜ **delay by two days only**：只延遲了2天、只耽誤2天

介系詞用 by

Fortunately, the shipment to Oscar Systems delayed by two days only.

幸好出給 Oscar Systems 的貨只耽誤了 2 天。

㉝ **production line**：生產線

I'm sorry, Jack. Our production lines are overloaded already. We don't have any extra capacity.

抱歉，Jack，我們的產線已經超載，沒有額外產能了。

㉞ **return from**：從…回來

My boss just returned from an overseas trip to U.K..

我老闆剛從英國出差回來。

㉟ **in fact**：事實上，也可說 **as a matter of fact**

If fact, we received fewer returns this year than last year.

事實上，我們今年收到的退貨比去年少。

NOTE

36 **it sounds good to me**：聽起來不錯

多用於回應他人，類似還有 It sounds interesting.（聽起來挺有趣）；It sounds great.（聽起來很讚）；也可省去 "It" 如 Sounds weird.（聽起來很怪異）

37 **in the end**：到後來

Believe me, Sandra. The investment in upgrading customer service will definitely pay off in the end.

相信我，Sandra。在提升客戶服務上的投資到後來必定能得到回報的。

38 **come up with**：產生、做出

Frank, I'm going to hang up now as I'll have to come up with a new product proposal by 9:00 later today.

Frank，我得掛斷了。今天稍晚 9:00 我還得提出一份新產品提案。

39 **covering**：涵蓋、包含

Our sales jurisdiction is fairly wide covering the entire west Pacific Rim and two Oceanian countries, namely Australia and New Zealand.

我們的業務範圍相當廣，涵蓋了整個西太平洋沿岸及大洋洲的澳洲和紐西蘭。

40 **relevant**：相關的、相對應的

Susan, please make sure that you send the meeting minutes to the relevant attendees.

Susan，請務必將會議紀錄傳給相關的與會者。

㊶ available：完成的、可用的

Jimmy, I'll see if we still have anything available for your urgent inquiry.

Jimmy，我來看看是否還有庫存可以緊急提供給你。

㊷ has been … already：最常見的現在完成進行式句型，表示至今還在進行動作

Becky has been with Pinnacle Control for more than 20 years already.

Becky 在 Pinnacle Control 工作已經超過 20 年了（現今依然在）。

㊸ nightmare：噩夢、夢魘

It has been a nightmare to me since Reddings Automation sued us for breach of contract.

自從 Readings Automation 告我們違約以來，我就一直做噩夢。

㊹ brief introduction：簡短介紹

Jane is going to give us a brief introduction on the new return handling procedures.

Jane 即將簡短介紹新退貨處理程序。

㊺ put into force：執行、使用

The 8D program was officially put into force company-wide early this week.

本週稍早，公司正式全面使用 8D 問題解決程序。

NOTE

㊻ within：在…之內

Alex, we need to finish the temperature tests within the time frame according to the QA procedure.

Alex，我們得依照QA程序，在規定的時間內完成溫度測試。

㊼ serve to：用來、拿來

The 8D report sent to customers serves to give a comprehensive explanation, from the root cause to the solutions of the incident.

交給客戶的 8D 報告，能針對事件從起因到結尾，提出全面性說明。

㊽ on a daily basis：按照每一天

Hans, concerning your performance, I'll monitor your progress through CRM on a daily basis.

Hans，關於你的業績，我會透過CRM每天監督你的進度。

㊾ go ahead：繼續、去做

You may want to go ahead and finish it in time.

你繼續把工作及時完成吧！

㊿ I'm not following you：我聽不懂你說的

I'm sorry, Kim. I'm not following you. Would you please say that again?

抱歉，Kim。我聽不懂你說的，能麻煩你再說一次好嗎？

51 being implemented：正（被）執行、實施

A new CRM system is being implemented in the sales department.

業務部正在跑一套新 CRM 系統。

52 company-wide：全公司

There will be a company-wide emergency drill tomorrow afternoon.

明天下午會有一場全公司的緊急應變演練。

53 stand for：代表

Arthur, what does RMA stand for?

Arthur，RMA 代表什麼？

54 tell from：從……明白了解

You may tell from Lisa's red eyes that she worked too hard.

從 Lisa 血紅的雙眼，你就知道她工作太認真了。

55 problem solving system：問題解決制度

A problem solving system such as 8D is very helpful to the salespeople.

像 8D 這種問題解決制度，對業務人員很有幫助。

56 go into details：敘述細節、討論細項

I'm not going into details as we only have half an hour.

因為我們只有半小時，我就不再敘述細項了。

NOTE

57 a lot easier：更容易，也可說 **much easier**

It will be a lot easier to do the reverse engineering than to design from scratch.

逆向工程要比從零開始設計簡單多了。

58 focus on：專注、集中注意

Ted, I think we should focus more on profitability than on revenues.

Ted，我認為我們應當更專注在獲利而不是在營收上。

59 core concept：核心概念

The core concept of B2B sales falls on building up long-term customer relationships.

B2B 業務的核心概念在於建立長期客戶關係。

60 in brief：簡短來說

In brief, we don't sell cheap.

一句話，我們價格不便宜。

61 further：更進一步的

I have no further comments.

我沒有更進一步的評論。

62 real quick：快快地

Mr. Lin, I'll send you the RMA number real quick.

林先生，我會快快傳 RMA 編號給你。

63 deal with：處理、對待

Emily, I want you to be more careful while dealing with customer complaints.

Emily，我要妳在處理客訴時更加小心些。

文重點① **Summary 1**

In the era of competition as of today, customer service, CS, has become an important competitive advantage for all business entities. It creates added value to the customers in more of a professional way. Particularly in B2B mode, customer service forms a reliable and long-term customer value. Providing customers with technical support has become one of the most effective ways in winning business on a long-term basis. Technical support requires investment in product technology, application engineering, as well as human resource. It will not be cheap. However, most of the time it pays off as it helps customers improve their products. In the long run, the customers rely on such technical support more so that it forms a valuable competitive edge against competitors.

當今企業，無不處心積慮想在各產業中勝出，客戶服務水平迅速成為差異化的主角，在企業經營成長策略中的重要性日益升高。特別是在 B2B 模式裡，技術支援能力往往扮演著關鍵的致勝角色。企業投資技術支援的資本支出，包含了產品科技、應用工程及人力資源，投資金額多半很高，不過由於能夠有效幫助客戶改善其產品，長期下來，客戶逐漸依賴這種技術支援，也就能夠形成一項競爭優勢，更是一項不易模仿複製的競爭策略。

 技術服務　Technical Support 7-1

 **Bill**：**Buyer, Baxton Computer (China)** 採購

 **Grace**：**Customer Service, Ultimate Cleaning (Taiwan)** 客服

Bill：Hi, this is Bill Harden from Baxton Computer. I'd like to speak to Art Stevens.

嗨，我是 Baxton　Computer 的 Bill　Harden。我想找 Art Stevens。

Grace：Hi, Bill. This is Grace Page. I'm the customer service contact of the sales department. I'm sorry Art is away on the road all day today. How may I help you?

嗨 Bill，我是 Grace Page，業務部門的客服專員。不好意思，Art 今天一整天都在外面忙，我能替你服務嗎？

Bill：We just found one of the new ultrasonic cleaners you installed last week not working well.

剛才我們發現一臺上星期才安裝的超音波清洗機不正常。

Grace：That's bad news. I'm very sorry to hear it. Would you mind telling me a bit more of the detail?

那真糟糕，非常抱歉。能麻煩你告訴我更多細節嗎？

Bill：OK, the machine vibrated badly and there's very loud noise coming out. It's kind of scary.

好。這臺機器晃得很厲害，而且會發出很大的噪音，有點恐怖。

Grace: I see. Do you know the serial number of this machine?

了解。你知道這臺機器的序號嗎？

Bill: Yes, I do. It is 7866-AX-21009.

知道，是 7866-AX-21009。

Grace: Very good, thanks. I'm going to ask our service engineer to contact you as quickly as possible.

太好了！謝謝。我會請我們維修工程師儘快和你連絡。

Bill: Grace, please treat this as an urgent case, OK?

Grace，麻煩妳儘快處理，好嗎？

Grace: Sure, I will. It won't take more than 5 minutes. And thanks for your patience.

當然，不會超過五分鐘，感謝你的耐心。

NOTE

① era：年代、時代

The traditional industries are in an era of quick shake-out.

傳統產業正處於一個快速淘汰的時代。

② as of today：到今天

As of today, we've been outperforming our competitors mainly by providing timely applications support.

到今天，我們主要靠著及時提供應用支援來打敗競爭對手。

③ customer service：客戶服務

It doesn't cost too much to establish an effective customer service system.

不需要花大錢，就能建立起一套有效的客戶服務系統。

④ competitive advantage：競爭優勢

For many years we've been able to maintain a market leader position with our technical support capability as a competitive advantage.

多年來，我們一直用技術支援能力當作一項競爭優勢，維持我們市場龍頭的地位。

⑤ business entity：企業體

B2B or B2B2C, sales is always the most important function in a private business entity.

無論 B2B 或 B2B2C，業務永遠是私人企業最重要的功能。

⑥ added value：增值、附加價值

From the customer's point of view, quality customer service can be a precious added value to the company.

從客戶角度來看，高品質的客戶服務是一項珍貴的企業附加價值。

⑦ more of：更加

Bill is more of an applications engineer than an R&D engineer.

與其說 Bill 是位研發工程師，還不如說他更像是應用工程師。

⑧ professional：專業的

I was impressed by Ian's professional approach in solving our technical problems.

我對 Ian 以專業方法解決我們技術上的問題，印象深刻極了。

NOTE

⑨ B2B mode：B2B 模式

Sales operations in B2B mode are much more complicated than that of B2C mode.

B2B 模式的業務操作比 B2C 複雜多了。

⑩ form：形成、構成

Our excellent online technical support and customer service form a special type of company resource.

我們超人一等的線上技術服務和客戶服務，構成了特殊的公司資源。

⑪ reliable：可靠的、可信賴的

Cosmos Trading is one of our most reliable distributors worldwide.

Cosmos Trading 是我們全球最可信賴的代理商之一。

⑫ customer value：客戶價值

Competitive price, short lead time, and consistent product quality are the core of our customer value.

具競爭力的價格、夠短的交期、以及一致的產品品質是我們客戶價值的核心。

⑬ provide … with …：用…提供給…

Most of the time, our FAEs would work with the users side by side doing troubleshooting and then provide them with recommendations if necessary.

我們應用工程師們多半會和現場使用單位一起偵錯，如果有必要，會再提供客戶建議事項。

⑭ effective：有效的

Recently, providing user customers with applications contents in the forms of e-books and online white papers has been proved quite effective.

近來用電子書及線上白皮書形式提供客戶應用內容，是一種相當有效的方法。

⑮ win business：贏得訂單、生意

In order to win more business from VAB, we will have to invest a lot more in marketing.

為了多拿 VAB 的生意，我們得在行銷上擴大投資。

⑯ product technology：產品科技

Whether we'll win the war or not depends largely on how advanced our product technology is.

究竟我們能否贏得戰爭，多半得看我們的產品科技有多先進。

⑰ application engineering：應用工程

In order to stay ahead of competition, we continue to invest heavily in application engineering as well as product engineering.

為了保持競爭優勢，我們持續大規模地投資在應用工程和產品工程上。

NOTE

⑱ **as well as**：和、以及

Our chief application engineer as well as I myself went to the site to check the damage as a result of the lightning.

我們的主任應用工程師和我趕到現場，查看雷擊所產生的損壞。

⑲ **human resource**：人力資源，指人才招募聘用

One of the problems we have in building up our application engineering team is human resource, i.e., recruiting experienced engineers.

在建立應用工程團隊過程中，我們遭遇到的諸多問題之一是人力資源。也就是招募到有經驗的工程師。

⑳ **cheap**：廉價、便宜

We don't sell cheap products to customers. We sell good products instead.

我們不賣廉價產品，而是賣好產品給客戶。

㉑ **pay off**：有回報、收成

Michael's great efforts in developing new markets over the past years finally paid off.

Michael 過去多年來在開發新市場上的努力終於有了回報。

㉒ improve：改善、使更好

Sean worked very hard doing lots of tests and experiments trying to improve the ovens along the production lines to get better performance.

Sean 非常努力地做了無數測試與實驗，試圖改善生產線上的烤箱，以增進運作效能。

㉓ in the long run：長遠來看、最後、到頭來

In the long run, customers will have to accept the GRI.

最後，客戶還是得接受 GRI。

GRI 為 General Rate Increase（全面性漲價）的縮寫

㉔ rely on：依靠、依賴

Our Y-T-D sales are lagging behind. We will have to rely on the launch of our new products next week.

目前我們業績落後，得依靠下星期的新產品發表了。

㉕ competitive edge：競爭優勢

It has been one of our competitive edges to provide customers with local technical service. And because of that, we've won a lot of unexpected orders.

提供在地技術服務一向是我們的競爭優勢之一，我們也因此拿到很多意外的訂單。

㉖ against：對抗、反對

Please bear in mind that we are now competing against those world-class companies like SSE and PAN.

請牢記，現今我們得和一些世界級的企業如 SSE 和 PAN 競爭。

NOTE

㉗ I'd like to：我想要

I'd like to emphasize that pricing won't be an issue. Instead, technical support is the key.

我想強調的是價格不是問題，技術服務才是關鍵。

㉘ on the road：在路上指出差在外

Charles has been on the road since two weeks ago.

Charles 已經出差在外二星期了。

㉙ all day today：今天一整天

Linda was ill all day today.

Linda 今天病了一整天。

㉚ how may I help you?：我能幫你什麼忙嗎？

是一句很有禮貌的常用對話，也可以說 How can I help you? 或 What can I do for you?

㉛ not work well：運作不理想、不正常

The new temperature chamber we installed last week was not working well.

我們上星期安裝的溫控箱運作不正常。

㉜ would you mind：請你（做某件事）

Do you mind ... 是指你介意我（做某件事）

Would you mind sending me the data sheet of your temperature chamber HL500?

請你傳你們溫控箱 HL500 的規格書給我好嗎？

Do you mind if I turn the air conditioner off while calibrating the balance?

當我在校正天平的時候，你介意我把空調關掉嗎？

㉝ a bit more：多一些，也可說 **a little bit more** 或 **a little more**

Currently profitability is a bit more important than revenues.

現階段，獲利比營收要來的更重要些。

㉞ vibrate：震動、顫動

We had to shut down one of our CNC machines which vibrated too much immediately after we powered it on.

我們得關掉那臺開機後震動過大的 CNC 加工機。

㉟ it's kind of scary：有些嚇人

kind of 是常用的口語說法，有些、有點的意思

I'm kind of tired.

我有點累了。

㊱ serial number：序號

Please send me the serial number of the machine so that I can issue an RMA number.

請將這臺機器的序號傳給我，以便開出 RMA 碼。

NOTE

㊲ treat … as：當作、看作

Our FAE team always treats customer's technical request as the number one priority.

我們應用工程團隊一向把客戶的技術要求當作首要處理事項。

㊳ urgent case：緊急個案、案件

The problem is being taken care of as an urgent case.

我們已經在緊急處理這個問題了。

文重點② Summary 2

To most industries, competing and growing business by providing customers with added value has proven to be more effective than any other form of competition such as pricing. It is because such value-added service helps customers make better products of their own. In the long run, it creates an unique value on which customers would constantly rely. For many industrial products, application support from manufacturers often plays a crucial role in the making of the purchasing decision by the buyers. As a result, more and more companies started to invest in application support. Most of the time they enjoy a higher ROI than they could get from many other marketing programs such as advertising and promotions. More often, we'll see FAE, field application engineers, are deployed in sales department. They work closely with the salespeople and also directly with the customers.

技術支援，更精確來說，應用支援，對於企業在當今產業競爭中勝出，或讓公司業績持續成長的功效，已經普遍受到肯定。無論高科技或傳統產業，產品除了本身技術規格外，使用單位的應用技術能力強弱，往往影響到最終產品的特性與品質。因此供應廠商若能提供完整的產品應用資訊，將有助於買方更有效開發最終產品。換句話說，廠商的應用支援愈強，愈能協助客戶開發出更好的最終產品。藉由這種方式建立起的客戶關係，遠較以其他行銷（如降價）或業務（如交際應酬）方式所建立的關係來得可靠穩固。更重要的是，這會是一種長期的互信關係。當今多數企業裡，應用工程師往往直接隸屬於業務部門：他們與業務人員互動密切，甚至經常直接提供客戶所需的應用工程服務。當然，有更多的客戶採購單位，已經將廠商的應用技術服務列入關鍵採購考慮因素內。這種趨勢使得不少企業開始認真投資在提升應用技術服務水平上面。

應用技術支援 FAE Support 7-2

> **Bill** : **Buyer, Baxton Computer (China)** 採購
>
> **Art** : **Senior Account Manager, Ultimate Cleaning (Taiwan)** 資深客戶經理

Bill : Hi, this is Bill Harden from Baxton Computer. May I speak to Art Stevens?

嗨，我是 Baxton Computer 的 Bill Harden，我可以和 Art Stevens 說話嗎？

Dr. Lee 解析

這是最簡單、最常用的問法。

Art : This is he. Hey Bill, it's been a long time. How are you doing?

我就是 Art Stevens。嘿 Bill，好久沒連絡，你好嗎？

Dr. Lee 解析

與其用最熟悉的「Speaking」或「This is Art speaking」，這裡用「This is he」可起耳目一新之作用。而「it's been a long time」，代表相隔一段長時間，是「... it has been a long time since ...」的簡單表示法。

Bill：Just fine and thanks. Actually I've been trying to <u>reach you</u> <u>since</u> last Wednesday. You <u>seemed to be</u> always <u>busy on the road</u>.

我很好，Art，謝謝你。事實上，從上星期三開始，我就一直在找你。不過你似乎都忙著出差呢！

Dr. Lee 解析

Bill 表示，其實他一直在找 Art 卻未果。猜測 Art 都在外面忙著跑客戶，很難找到人。

Art：I'm very sorry about that. I've been so busy in recent weeks since one of my sales guys <u>became ill</u> <u>a couple of</u> weeks ago. What can I do for you today?

真是抱歉，最近幾星期我一直都很忙，因為我有位業務已掛病號兩星期了。今天是什麼事找我？

Dr. Lee 解析

業務人員最自然反應，對於讓客戶找不到人先表示抱歉，並簡單說明原因後，切入正題。

Bill：I really need your help this time. We are developing a new <u>automated packaging system</u> for the <u>food processing industry</u> and some <u>customized applications</u> with your newest digital <u>dampers</u>.

這回我真的要靠你幫忙了。公司正利用你們最新的數位阻尼傳感器，來開發一套新的自動包裝系統，給食品加工業者以及一些客製化應用。

Dr. Lee 解析

當客戶頭次使用供應商產品開發新系統時，最需要供應廠商提供足夠的技術或應用支援。

Art : That's very nice. I'm so glad that you would choose our digital dampers for your new systems. This will be the first time you use such high-speed sensors, right?

那太好了！真高興你們選擇我們的數位阻尼傳感器來開發新系統，這是你們頭一次使用這種高速傳感器吧？

Dr. Lee 解析

從業務觀點來看，客戶第一次選擇自家的產品開發新系統，應該是最高興的事了，非得好好把握住不可。

Bill : Yes. it is the first time for us. And that's why our R&D engineers asked me to provide them with <u>as much</u> technical information <u>as possible</u>. They need to do a number of <u>tests and experiments</u> with the dampers before <u>kicking off the project</u>.

是的，對我們來說，這是頭一次。也因此，我們研發工程師要我盡可能提供他們更多技術資料。在啟動這研發案前，他們得在這款傳感器上做各種測試和實驗。

Dr. Lee 解析

研發工程師們首當其衝，必須得經過測試與實驗確定可行後，才能進行正式作業。

Art : <u>Not a problem at all.</u> I'll talk with our applications engineers later today regarding your requirement for application support. <u>Very likely, I myself</u> and our application engineers will visit your R&D guys sometime next week.

沒問題。我稍晚會和我們的應用工程師討論你們這項應用支援的需求。可能在下週，我和應用工程師們會一起拜訪你們的研發工程師。

Dr. Lee 解析

有能力提供應用支援的廠商，最樂於收到客戶研發工程師所提出的支援要求。通常會由負責業務與應用工程師共同拜訪，開始進行了解與討論。

Bill : That's great. I'm sure that <u>not only</u> our R&D engineers, <u>but also</u> many of our top guys, would like to meet you <u>by then</u>.

那太好了！我相信到時不只是我們研發工程師，連很多大人物們都會來見你們的。

Dr. Lee 解析

全新開發案對於客戶必定是一項大事，供應廠商的應用支援也
會讓客戶特別關注的。

Art : Good, I'll do it right away. But before that, both of us have
something to work on.

好啊！我這就來安排。不過在那之前，你我都得先做些功課。

Dr. Lee 解析

正式開場前，業務與採購得先解決一些非技術性問題。

Bill : What do I need to do now?

那我現在得做什麼？

Art : You will have to pass a copy of the application questionnaire
on to your R&D engineer responsible for the new system. He
or she will have to fill it out with relevant data or information.
We need to receive the returned questionnaire ASAP.

你得將一份應用問卷交給負責新系統的研發工程師，等工程師
填好相關的數據或資訊後，儘快回傳給我。

Dr. Lee 解析

這供應廠商提供一份應用（技術）問卷，讓客戶研發或工程單
位填寫，以便初步決定可能的解決方案。

Bill : OK. I'll send it to him as soon as I receive it from you. What's the purpose of the questionnaire?

好的。一旦我收到問卷，就會馬上傳給他。這份問卷是做什麼的？

Dr. Lee 解析

採購負責轉交，並試圖了解問卷目的。

Art : It helps your engineers focus on the key system features critical to the selection of the digital dampers. It also gives our application engineer an overall understanding of your new system. In other words, the questionnaire serves as a technical platform on which we work together for a solution.

那問卷能幫助你們的工程師，專注在選用傳感器時要考慮的重要系統特性上。同時，也能夠讓我們應用工程師對這系統有整體的認識。換句話說，這份問卷成為我們彼此合作的技術平臺。

Dr. Lee 解析

該應用問卷有雙重目的。其一是協助客戶研發工程師，了解並專注於廠商產品的特性，並與新系統開發做整體技術思考，另一目的，則是讓應用工程師對於客戶新系統有整體了解，以便做出最適當解決方案。

Bill : Wow, I learned quite a lot from you today. Now I understand how important it is to receive good technical support from the supplier when there's a new project coming up.

哇！我今天從你這裡學到很多。現在我了解能得到廠商優質的技術服務有多重要了，特別是當有新的研發案要進行時。

Dr. Lee 解析

不經一事，不長一智。連採購都能學到不少技術和應用的常識。

Art : My pleasure. It always feels great to know we grow with our customers by helping them make better products.

那是我的榮幸。知道公司能幫助客戶做出更好的產品，進而和客戶一起成長，那種感覺非常棒。

Dr. Lee 解析

業務最樂意見到的是，能幫助客戶使用自家產品，生產出優良最終產品。兩相得利，形成雙贏局面。

NOTE

① prove：證明、證實

Larry's excellent performance has proven that he's capable of becoming a B2B salesperson.

Larry 的優秀表現證明了他有能力成為一位 B2B 業務人員。

② effective：有效的

We were requested by the management to be more effective in developing new business for the group.

管理階層要求我們得更有效地替集團開發新生意。

③ pricing：定價

Competing solely by pricing can be dangerous.

只靠價格來競爭是很危險的。

④ value-added：附加價值

The value-added service provided by the channel partners is important to both the manufacturer and the end customer.

通路夥伴所提供的加值服務，對廠商及終端客戶都很重要。

⑤ of their own：他們自己的

After all the hard work in applications service over the past years, they finally built up a reputation of their own.

憑著過去幾年在應用工程服務上的努力，他們終於建立起自己的信譽。

⑥ **unique**：獨特的、獨有的

Our relationship with Taiwan Steel is pretty unique.

我們和 Taiwan Steel 的關係相當獨特。

⑦ **on which customers would constantly rely**：

也可說成"**which customers would constantly rely on**"介系詞 **on** 緊接在動詞 **rely** 之後。

⑧ **play a crucial role**：扮演著關鍵角色

play a role 指扮演一種角色

Stanley has been playing a crucial role in our sales team for a long time.

長期以來，Stanley 在我們業務團隊中，一直扮演一個關鍵角色。

⑨ **as a result**：因此、結果

Eric failed to finish the PowerPoint stuff in time. As a result, the meeting was postponed to late afternoon.

Eric 沒能及時完成 Power Point 製作，因此會議延後到今天下午。

⑩ **more and more**：愈來愈多

More and more salespeople rely on CRM system to improve work efficiency.

愈來愈多業務人員依賴 CRM 系統來改善工作效率。

NOTE

⑪ **ROI**：投資報酬率，是 **Return On Investment** 的縮寫

Nowadays, even salespeople are evaluated by all kinds of ROI.

現今，即使是業務人員的績效，也是以各種投資報酬率來評核。

⑫ **more often**：經常、時常

More often, the customers complained about poor after-sale service.

客戶經常抱怨售後服務很差。

⑬ **deploy**：配置、部署

Since they are so important to us, we have deployed a dedicated FAE to serve them.

由於他們的重要性，我們配了一位專屬 FAE 服務他們。

⑭ **this is he**：我就是（他，Art）

也可說 "This is Art." 或 "This is Art speaking."，或者更簡潔直接說 "Speaking"

⑮ **it's been a long time**：已經好久（不見、未說過話）

It's been 是 it has been 的縮寫

NOTE

⑯ **I've been trying … since**：自從…以來我一直
"**have been** + 動詞進行式 + **since**"之後要以過去時間
點來表示

Francis has been working on Ace Metal since last February.

Francis 自從二月開始就一直在開發 Ace Metal。

⑰ **reach you**：找到你、聯絡到你

Joseph was busy trying to reach his assistant when his number
one account Jupiter Precision called.

當 Joseph 的最大客戶 Jupiter Precision 打電話來時，他正忙
著聯絡他的助理。

⑱ **seem to be**：似乎、看起來

My boss seemed to be in good mood when he stepped in the
office earlier this morning.

今天稍早我老闆進辦公室時心情似乎很好。

⑲ **busy on the road**：出差在外忙

I'm sorry. Julie is busy on the road. May I take the message?

很抱歉，Julie 出差在外，您能留話嗎？

⑳ **become ill**：生病了

Unfortunately Mandy became ill today and could not attend the
sales meeting.

很不幸，Mandy 今天病了，無法參加業務會議。

NOTE

21 a couple of：二個、二種、幾個

Because of the materials shortage, we'll have to wait for a couple of more weeks.

由於原物料短缺，我們得再等幾週。

22 automated packaging system：自動包裝系統。

An automated packaging system plays an important role in an integrated manufacturing system.

自動包裝系統在整合製造系統中扮演著重要角色。

23 food processing industry：食品加工產業

Hygiene issues can do serious harm to the food processing industry.

衛生問題會帶給食品加工業嚴重傷害。

24 customized applications：客製化應用

The customized applications business generated much more profits than the standard applications.

客製化應用生意利潤比標準應用生意高出許多。

25 damper：阻尼傳感器，是 **damped transducer** 的簡稱

Dampers are commonly found in dynamic automation applications.

在動態自動化應用裡，經常會用到阻尼傳感器。

㉖ as much … as possible：儘可能多

We were requested by the headquarters to provide as much competitor information as possible prior to the national sales meeting.

總公司要求我們在全國業務會議前，儘可能提供更多競爭同行資訊。

㉗ test and experiment：測試與實驗

Our R&D engineers are doing numerous tests and experiments on the crystal oscillators selected for the new projects.

我們研發工程師正在為新研發案選購的石英震盪器，做許多測試與實驗。

㉘ kick off the project：啓動專案

After kicking off the project, Danny immediately hold a project meeting with the responsible engineers.

啓動專案後，Danny 立即和負責的工程師們開專案會議。

㉙ not a problem at all：完全沒問題，同 No problem at all

㉚ very likely：很可能

It is very likely that we will be able to hit the target by the end of the year.

到年底我們很可能會達成目標。

NOTE

③① **I myself**：我自己，強調語氣

I myself will attend the project meeting this afternoon.

我會參加今天下午的專案會議。

③② **not only … but also …**：不但…而且…

The ambient vibration will affect not only the accuracy but also the operating life of the system.

周遭環境的震動，不但會影響系統精確度，還會影響系統壽命。

③③ **by then**：屆時、到時候

Don't worry, Greg. We'll deliver the replacement to you by then.

別擔心，Greg，到時候我們會將替換品交到你手上。

③④ **before that**：在那之前

We'll have a conference call with Marvin's team tomorrow. Before that, we need to finish our jobs.

我們明天將和 Marvin 的團隊開視訊會議，在那之前，得先完成自己的工作。

③⑤ **work on**：努力做、致力於

Let's finish the meeting quicker as we still have ton of stuff to work on.

我們得快點結束會議，因為還有成堆的事情得做。

NOTE

㊱ **pass … on to (someone)**：傳給某人、轉給某人。

Please pass the samples on to Jessy for me.

請幫我把這些樣品轉交給 Jessy。

㊲ **application questionnaire**：應用問卷

Please fill out the application questionnaire and send it to me ASAP.

請填好這份應用問卷後儘快回傳給我。

㊳ **responsible for**：為…負責

Bob is the guy responsible for the Seton project.

Bob 負責 Seton 專案。

㊴ **relevant**：相關的、有關的。

Kim, after our conversation, please make sure to send me the relevant stats by e-mail.

Kim，等我們通完話，請務必把相關統計資料用 e-mail 傳給我。

㊵ **returned**：返回的、回覆的

Please confirm acceptable by returned e-mail.

請以 e-mail 回覆可接受。

㊶ **as soon as**：一…就…

Cindy, I'll call you as soon as I've landed at San Francisco airport.

Cindy，等飛機一降落舊金山機場，我就打電話給妳。

NOTE

㊷ purpose：目的

The main purposes of the 8D report are to identify the cause of the problem, rectify it, and then make sure it won't happen again.

8D 報告最主要目的在於找出問題點加以改正，並確保同樣問題不再發生。

㊸ focus on：專注在

Sara, you need to focus on getting more high-margin orders.

Sara，妳得專注在拿更多高毛利的訂單。

㊹ key system features：重要系統特性

High speed and high accuracy are the key system features of this automatic checking machine.

高速與高精確度是這套自動分檢機的重要系統特性。

㊺ critical to：對⋯重要

A well-planned visiting schedule is critical to a traveling salesperson.

對經常出差的業務人員來說，一份規劃周詳的拜訪行程是很重要的。

㊻ overall understanding：整體性理解

Being a B2B sales, you need to have an overall understanding of customer's applications requirements.

身為 B2B 業務，你得對客戶的應用需求有整體性的了解。

47 in other words：換言之、換句話說

Customer may call you anytime in a day. In other words, you have to be on call 24 hours a day.

客戶任何時間都可能打電話找你，換句話說，你得 24 小時待命。

48 technical platform：技術平臺

We provide our customers with an excellent technical platform with which they develop their products.

我們提供客戶一個很棒的技術平臺讓他們開發產品。

49 quite a lot：相當多、很多

Denise knows quite a lot of our suppliers as she used to be a purchaser in one of our competitors.

Denise 認識相當多供應廠商，因為她先前在我們一家對手公司擔任採購。

50 come up：想出、提出

If you ever come up with any better idea, be sure to tell me ASAP.

如果你想出任何更好的點子，請務必盡早告訴我。

51 my pleasure：我的榮幸，也是「不客氣」的另一種說法

52 feel great：感覺很棒

It feels great to win back such a big order.

能奪回如此大訂單感覺真棒。

NOTE

⑤③ grow with：和…一起成長

The best way to grow yourself as a sales professional is to grow with your customers.

業務追求專業成長最好的方式，就是和客戶一起成長。

⑤④ by：藉由

We're going to help you solve the problems by offering our design drawings.

我們會藉由提供我們的設計圖來協助你們解決問題。

Lesson 8 應收帳款
Accounts Receivable

課文重點① Summary 1

Collection is just too important to ignore while running a business of any size. To a salesperson, making sure that customers pay in time and in full is as important as getting orders from the customers. Very often, however, salespeople tend to miss the point and are unable to act proactively. When it happens, overdue accounts or even bad debts could do serious harm to the business. Therefore, accounts receivable has become one of the KPIs of a salesperson.

一個完整的銷售流程，是以銷售貨款及時入帳才算結束。因此，對於業務人員來說，接單只是起頭而已，還得持續專注確保及時收齊貨款。當下各型企業，多半都借助 ERP 系統財會模組中應收帳款功能，定期提供業務單位相關資訊以利管理。然而，在實務上，逾期款依舊時時發生，這對於企業資金運用極為不利，就更不用說發生壞帳的後果了。因此，越來越多企業對於自家業務團隊的績效評核，已經將應收款責任權重大幅提高，重要性可與接單出貨平起平坐。

應收帳款 1　Accounts Receivable 1 8-1

Jenny：**Account Manager, Stars Technology (Taiwan)** 客戶
經理

David：**Purchaser, Wonder Clean Inc. (Australia)** 採購

Jenny：Hi David, this is Jenny Walker of Stars Technology. How are you doing today?

嗨 David。我是 Stars Technology 的 Jenny Walker，你今天好嗎？

David：Just fine, thank you. How about you?

我很好，謝謝。那妳呢？

Jenny：Good. Remember the shipment of 10 machines we made to you in May?

我很好。你還記得我們在五月份出給你們那 10 臺機器的貨嗎？

David：Sure, what about it?

我記得，怎麼了？

Jenny：Our accounts lady told me that you hadn't paid yet. It's already overdue.

我們會計小姐告訴我，你們還沒付款喔！它已經逾期了。

David：What! <u>Still not been paid?</u> I'm very sorry. I'll check with our accounts department <u>real quick</u> and <u>call you back later</u>.

什麼？還沒付啊？真是抱歉。我這就去會計部快快查一下，稍晚回你電話。

Jenny：Thanks, David.

謝謝，David。

(later...)

David：Hi Jenny, this is David. Regarding the overdue account, we are very sorry that something <u>went wrong</u> when our bank tried to <u>remit</u> the money to you. I'd like to <u>apologize to</u> you for <u>the mistake</u>. And we will <u>pay by wire</u> this afternoon.

嗨 Jenny，我是 David。關於那筆逾期貨款，真是抱歉，銀行在匯款時出了點錯，我在這兒向你們道歉。我們今天下午就去電匯。

Jenny：<u>That's all right.</u> I'm glad <u>things are clear</u> now. Thanks.

沒關係，很高興事情解決了，多謝嘍！

1 accounts receivable：應收帳款，常用 **AR** 縮寫表示

Mark, you need to trim your AR right away as many are already overdue.

Mark，你得立即減低你應收款，有好多都已經逾期了。

NOTE

② collection：收款

To a B2B sales, collection is as important, if not more, as getting orders.

對 B2B 業務人員來說，即使不敢說收款比接單重要，至少要說二者同等重要。

③ run a business：經營一家企業、公司

It takes both aggressiveness and conservativeness while running a business.

經營企業，既要積極進取，也須保守謹慎。

④ of any size：任何一種規模

Staying competitive to grow is essential to any business of any size.

無論規模大小，企業要成長就一定得具備競爭力。

⑤ in time：及時

We were able to ship the goods to Ampex Tools yesterday afternoon as they finally cleared the overdue payments in time.

由於 Ampex Tools 終於及時付清逾期款項，我們昨天下午才能把貨出給他們。

⑥ in full：全部、全額

Alex, you must check carefully to make sure they have paid in full.

Alex，你一定得查清楚，確定他們已經全額付清了。

NOTE

⑦ get orders：拿訂單

Being a born B2B sales, nothing in the world will keep me from getting orders.

身為天生的 B2B 業務人員，世間沒有任何事能阻止我去拿訂單。

⑧ tend to：傾向

Some of our customers tend to pay us late.

有些客戶往往會延遲付款。

⑨ miss the point：沒抓到重點

I think you missed the point, Mike. Currently we have to focus on Tier 1 customers.

Mike，我認為你沒抓到重點，現階段我們得集中精神在第一階客戶上。

⑩ proactively：有前瞻性地、積極主動地

Cindy, as a customer service person, you'd better think and act proactively for our customers.

Cindy，身為客服人員，你最好要用前瞻性思考、積極及作為來服務我們的客戶。

⑪ overdue accounts：逾期帳款

Top management requested us to slash the overdue accounts to less than 5% of the total AR amount.

管理高層要求我們將逾期貨款金額比例減至低於 5%。

NOTE

⑫ **bad debts**：壞帳

Jeremy, I have zero tolerance for any bad debts. So do whatever you should do to eliminate them.

Jeremy，我不容許任何壞帳發生，所以你得竭盡所能地消除壞帳。

⑬ **do serious harm to**：造成嚴重傷害

Robin, your negligence in collection has done serious harm to the company.

Robin，你收款上的疏失已嚴重傷害到公司了。

⑭ **KPIs**：關鍵績效指標，**Key Performance Indicators** 的縮寫

Julie, apart from those sales-oriented KPIs, would you please pay more attention to the AR?

Julie，除了那些銷售相關的關鍵績效指標之外，請妳多注意應收帳款好嗎？

⑮ **shipment … made to you**：出給你們的貨

Andy, we forgot to include the invoice in the master carton of the shipment we made to you last Friday.

Andy，上星期五出給你們那筆貨，我們忘了隨貨發票。

⑯ **what about it**：怎麼了呢

NOTE

⑰ **accounts lady**：會計部小姐

One of our accounts ladies told me that she received a bad check from our bank drawn by Gibons Steel.

我們一位會計小姐告訴我，她從銀行那裡收到 Gibons Steel 開的一張空頭支票。

⑱ **hadn't paid yet**：尚未付款

否定句的「尚未」用「yet」

I didn't notice that York Machinery hadn't paid yet.

我沒注意 York Machinery 還沒付款。

⑲ **already overdue**：已經逾期

Abby, do you know two out of the three ARs of Ajax Automation are already overdue?

Abby，妳知道嗎？Ajax Automation 的三筆應收款中有二筆已經逾期了。

⑳ **still not been paid?**：仍然還沒付清嗎？

Sabrina, are you saying that all the four overdue accounts of Dexter Tooling still haven't been paid?

Sabrina，妳是說 Dexter Tooling 的四筆逾期款都還沒付清嗎？

NOTE

㉑ accounts department：會計部

I guess the accounts department of every company has the same working principle, i.e., "making no mistakes".

我猜每家公司的會計部門都有相同的工作準則，那就是「零錯誤」。

㉒ real quick：快快地

Wendy, we're going to remit you the money for invoice number RL201752 real quick.

Wendy，我們會快快匯款付清發票號碼 RL201752 的那筆貨款。

㉓ call you back later：稍後回電給你

I'm sorry Larry. I got to leave now. I'll call you back later from the airport.

對不起 Larry。我現在得離開了，稍後到機場回電給你。

㉔ go wrong：出錯

As of now, we are still trying to find out what went wrong with our AP system.

到現在，我們還在試著找出應付帳款系統到底出了什麼錯。

㉕ remit：匯出

Eugene, please make sure that we remit money to Sunden Crystals this morning to clear the overdue accounts.

Eugene，請務必在今早匯款給 Sunden Crystals，把逾期貨款清掉。

NOTE

㉖ **apologize for the mistake**：為犯錯道歉

Becky, I'd like to apologize to you for the mistake we made with the recent shipment.

Becky，我對最近出貨上的失誤向妳們道歉。

㉗ **pay by wire**：以電匯付款

Norah, I'm going to pay by wire later today.

Norah，我今天稍晚就電匯付款。

㉘ **that's all right**：沒關係

㉙ **things are clear**：事情解決了

Guys, now that things are clear, why not let's go have a beer?

各位，既然事情解決了，大家一起去喝杯啤酒吧！

課文重點② **Summary 2**

The AR <u>performance</u> is one of the KPIs of a salesperson. It <u>ties directly to</u> a salesperson's <u>sales commission</u>. <u>On the other hand</u>, payment <u>punctuality</u> is extremely important to a buyer as it ties directly to the <u>payment terms</u> as well as the <u>discount</u> the selling company is <u>willing to offer</u>. Therefore, it is the <u>responsibility</u> of both parties to make sure that payment is made <u>on time</u>.

應收帳款是業務人員的 KPI 之一，收款直接影響到業務佣金的多寡。這對業務人員來說非常重要，不可掉以輕心。另一方面從客戶端來說，貨款支付的情形也直接影響到客戶的信用與價格折扣。對於付款紀錄不佳的客戶，廠商往往不會考慮任何價格或付款條件上的優惠。因此廠商業務和客戶採購都必須特別留意準時收款付款。

 應收帳款 2　Accounts Receivable 2　🎧 8-2

😊 Jenny ：**Account Manager, Stars Technology (Taiwan)** 客戶
經理

😊 David ：**Purchaser, Wonder Clean Inc. (Australia)** 採購

😊 Jenny ：Hi David, this is Jenny Walker of Stars Technology. <u>How are you doing?</u>

嗨 David，我是 Stars Technology 的 Jenny Walker，你好嗎？

Dr. Lee 解析

很常見的問候語。

😊 David ：Hi Jenny, just fine, <u>pretty busy though</u>. How about yourself?

嗨 Jenny。我很好啊！不過非常忙就是了。妳呢？

Dr. Lee 解析

這裡用了以連接詞 though 為句尾的說法：pretty busy though，是口語英文裡常用的說法，though 連接前後二個句子：「我很好，但很忙。」

Jenny ： Me too, very busy. I need to <u>bring this to your personal attention</u>. It's about your payment records.

我也是忙壞了。我得提醒你特別注意一件事，就是關於你們的付款記錄。

切入重點談付款紀錄，並請對方特別留意。

David ： It <u>sounds rather serious</u>. <u>I haven't paid too much attention to it</u> <u>for a while</u>. Is there <u>anything wrong with</u> our payment？

聽起來好像很嚴重，我也有一陣子沒特別注意我們付款的事了，是出了什麼錯嗎？

也聽出來事件嚴重性，再度確認問題所在。

Jenny ： You <u>haven't been</u> able to pay us on time <u>since</u> last May. Our records showed that you were always <u>late by 7 to 10 days</u> for <u>each and every</u> account payable.

自從五月份以來，你們都不曾準時付款，每次都晚了 7 至 10 天左右。

Dr. Lee 解析

以確切數據告知拖延付款的問題。

David：I'm very sorry to hear that, Jenny. I <u>had an impression</u> that we paid late for a few times <u>as a result of</u> <u>bank change</u> during that period. I thought things <u>went back to normal</u> after <u>a short while</u>.

聽妳這麼說，我真感到抱歉。我有印象那段時間裡，因為換銀行的關係，我們曾經遲付過幾次，但是我以為不久後就已經恢復正常了。

Dr. Lee 解析

商場常識：說話禮節還是很重要。這種情況下，若能先表示歉意，將會使通話氣氛緩和許多。接著主事者說明自身所掌握的資訊。

Jenny：I'm afraid <u>that's not the case</u>. And because of such frequent delay, we will have to change your payment period from existing <u>Net 60</u> to <u>Paid Up Front</u>. The <u>dealer discount</u> will also change if it continues.

事實恐怕不是那樣。由於這麼經常延遲付款，我們得將你們現在的 60 天付款期改為款到出貨。而且如果情況持續，你們經銷商折扣也會改的。

Dr. Lee 解析

當然事實並非那樣。賣方得將延遲付款的嚴重後果清楚告訴對方（多會以電郵作為正式紀錄）。這裡不但付款期限會變，連同經銷折扣也可能更改。

David: I know it was our mistake paying too late. Please trust me that I'll <u>get it right</u> immediately after our conversation.

Jenny，我了解延遲付款是我們的錯，不過請相信我一定在結束談話後馬上改正這狀況。

Dr. Lee 解析

身段語氣放低、放軟，有益無害。這麼嚴重的後果，對於公司營運影響很大。主事者要顯露出會立刻解決問題的姿態，好讓事件有商量轉圜的空間。

Jenny: I do trust you but this is the <u>instruction</u> I received from our top managers. Please try <u>to be in my shoes</u>. I really have no other <u>alternatives</u>.

我相信你沒問題，不過這是我們高層所下的指令。請你設身處地替我想想，我真的別無選擇。

Dr. Lee 解析

> 當然賣方站在出貨收款的生意立場，還是必須把話說清楚，請對方從同理心出發，體諒公司採取嚴厲懲罰性動作的原因。

David: I fully understand your position. And I do appreciate you told me now so that I can resolve it immediately. Jenny, please consider giving a second chance to us.

我完全理解妳的立場，也很感謝妳現在告訴我，讓我能馬上解決這問題。不過 Jenny，請考慮再給我們一次機會。

Dr. Lee 解析

> 看得出雙方還是有一定程度的買賣關係，而能相互體諒。此時是提出請求補救的好時機。

Jenny: Ok, David. Let me talk with my boss first and I'll call you later this afternoon.

好，David，先讓我和老闆談談。我下午回你電話。

Dr. Lee 解析

> 如此事情有所轉圜。

David : Thank you so much. I'll be around for the rest of the day.

真是感謝。我整個下午都會在公司的。

Dr. Lee 解析

表示隨時等候通知。

(later...)

Jenny : Hello David, my boss accepted my suggestion to keep your present payment term on condition that you pay in time in the future.

哈囉 David，我們老闆接受我的建議，維持你們現在的付款方式，先決條件是你們未來一定得及時付款。

Dr. Lee 解析

還是不忘提及自己在事件當中的努力，讓對方了解。

David : Thanks very much for your help. I'm going to hold a meeting with our accounts department in an hour to make sure we do it right from now on.

多謝妳的幫忙。再過一小時，我就和會計部門開會，確保未來準時付款。

Dr. Lee 解析

除了致謝之外，立刻告訴對方即將採取措施改正。

Jenny ：That's great, and I'm glad we <u>sorted this out</u> today.
那太棒了！很高興我們今天就搞定這件事。

Dr. Lee 解析

雙方努力的結果。

NOTE

❶ **performance**：業績、績效、表現

Janet, your overall performance in the past six months was not very satisfactory.

Janet，妳過去半年的整體業績不是太令人滿意。

❷ **tie directly to**：與⋯相關聯

Pete, you'd better do something about your stock level quickly as it ties directly to your sales commission.

Pete，你最好快點降低你的庫存水準，因為那會直接影響到你的銷售佣金。

NOTE

❸ **sales commission**：銷售佣金

Our HR uses a very sophisticated formula to calculate the sales commission and bonus as well.

我們人資用一套很複雜的公式來計算銷售佣金和分紅。

❹ **on the other hand**：另一方面

Mr. Wang, we are forced to change your payment period to Net 30 as a result of the incident. On the other hand, your discount has been cancelled too.

王先生，由於這事件，我們被迫更改你們的付款期成為 Net 30。另一方面，你們的折扣也被取消了。

❺ **punctuality**：準時、守時

David, you can tell from your records that we have been keeping an excellent punctuality except for this time.

David，你能從紀錄上看出來，除了這一次，我們一向都非常準時。

❻ **payment terms**：付款條件

My boss asked me to send a formal notice to First Chemical that their payment terms will change starting July 1.

老闆要我傳正式通知給 First Chemical，將從 7 月 1 日開始變更他們的付款條件。

7 discount：折扣

Heidi, we're going to adjust your distributor discount from 20% to 30% as a consequence of the increased business volume last year.

Heidi，由於去年你們採購量大增，我們將把你們的代理商折扣從 20% 調高為 30%。

8 willing to：願意

Albert, if you increase our allocation to 33%, I'm willing to lower our quote by an additional 5%.

Albert，如果你把我們配額提高到 33%，我願意再降價 5%。

9 offer：提議、提供、出價、給予

Tom, our offer will be based on the business volume you're to commit in the next couple of years.

Tom，我們的提案是根據你們所承諾未來幾年的生意量來決定的。

10 responsibility：責任

It is the responsibility of a B2B salesperson to act as the interface between the customer and the company.

扮演好客戶與公司之間的溝通介面是一位 B2B 業務的責任。

11 on time：準時

Speaking of payment, I insist that we pay on time.

說起貨款，我很堅持我們必須準時付款。

NOTE

⓬ **how are you doing**：你好嗎？同 **How are you?** 或 **What's up?**

⓭ **pretty busy though**：但是很忙
口語上常把 though 放在句尾

A 3-day trip to Shanghai? Shoud be fun, pretty tight though.

三天的上海行程？應該很好玩，但是會很緊湊。

⓮ **bring this to your personal attention**：提出來好讓你特別注意

to one's attention 是指讓某人注意到

Victor, there's one thing I'd like to bring to your personal attention.

Victor，有件事我想請你特別注意。

⓯ **sounds rather serious**：聽起來相當嚴重

You said they cancelled the order? It sounds rather serious.

你是說他們取消訂單？聽起來挺嚴重的。

⓰ **I haven't paid too much attention to it**：我沒太注意這件事

pay attention to 指對…注意。用 much 而不說 many，因為 attention 不可數

I didn't pay too much attention to what he said about next year's budget.

我沒太注意他對於明年預算說了些什麼。

⑰ for a while：一段時間、一陣子

Mandy, what happened to BBT Automation? We haven't received their order for a while.

Mandy，BBT Automation 是怎麼了？有一陣子沒他們的單子了。

⑱ anything wrong with：（在某方面、某件事、或某個人）有什麼不對勁嗎？

Meggy, is there anything wrong with First Chemical? They paid late for the last two months.

Meggy，First Chemical 有什麼不對勁嗎？他們近二個月都延遲付款。

⑲ haven't been … since：自從…尚未

Mighty Tooling hasn't been trying to rebuild its sales team since Scott Chen's team left 3 months ago.

自從 Scott Chen 的團隊三個月前離職以來，Mighty Tooling 都還不曾試著重建業務團隊。

⑳ late by 7 to 10 days：遲了7至10天之久

Most of the time, Simon was late to work by 15 to 20 minutes.

Simon 上班多半會遲到 15 到 20 分鐘。

NOTE

㉑ each and every one：每一（有強調的意味）
一般用 each 或 every 就可以

Each and every one of our sales team received a fat bonus last year as a result of the outstanding performance.

由於去年業績非常優異，我們業務團隊每位成員都收到可觀的紅利。

㉒ have an impression：有印象

Rose, I had an impression that you went to Jakarta last summer to collect money from Indomachines.

Rose，我有印象妳去年夏天曾經去雅加達向 Indomachines 收貨款。

㉓ as a result of：由於、因為，也可用 **because of**

George decided to quit as a result of a prolonged health problem.

由於長期健康問題，George 決定辭職。

㉔ bank change：更換銀行

Mike, we need to inform our customers of the bank change.

Mike，我們得通知客戶匯款銀行變了。

㉕ go back to normal：恢復正常、恢復常態

Our day-to-day operations went back to normal after our budget period came to an end.

預算期告一段落，我們日常作業恢復正常了。

NOTE

㉖ a short while：一段短暫時間、短短一陣子
Our stock level was too high for a short while.
曾有一小段期間，我們庫存水準過高了。

㉗ I'm afraid …：恐怕…、抱歉…
Frank, I'm afraid that you'll have to deal with it by yourself.
抱歉，Frank，你得自己面對處理。
Bruce, I'm afraid that things are not as simple as you thought.
Bruce，事情恐怕不是你想像那麼單純。

㉘ that's not the case：（實情）並非如此
Chris, regarding layoff, the boss told me that's not the case.
Chris，關於資遣一事老闆告訴我並非如此。

㉙ existing：現行的、目前的
I guess the existing warranty period is not competitive enough.
我認為目前的保固期競爭力不夠。

㉚ Net 60：發票日期算起60天付清發票淨額（付款期）

㉛ Paid Up Front：款到出貨、預付現金

㉜ dealer discount：經銷商折扣，或說 reseller discount
We started to review the dealer discount in order to stay competitive.
我們已著手檢討經銷商折扣以保持競爭力。

NOTE

㉝ get it right：改正、糾正過來，或說 **rectify it**

There are too many mistakes in this spreadsheet. We'll have to get it right.

這張試算表錯誤太多了，我們得改正過來。

㉞ instruction：指示、指令，或說 **guidance**

Nancy, you should have received the instructions from the boss concerning the seminar next week.

Nancy，你應該已經收到老闆對下週研討會的指示了吧？

㉟ to be in my shoes：站在我的立場想，也可說 **put yourself in my shoes.**

Henry, please try to be in my shoes. It is my responsibility to protect our benefits.

Henry，請站在我的立場想，我有責任維護公司的利益。

㊱ alternatives：其他選擇、其他辦法，也可說 **choices** 或 **options**

Barry, it doesn't seem to be feasible. Do we have any alternatives?

Barry，那似乎不可行，有其他辦法嗎？

㊲ I'll be around：我都會在，不會外出的意思

Jackie, call me if you need me. I'll be around.

Jackie，如果有需要，儘管打電話，我都會在辦公室。

㊳ the rest of the day：今天剩下的時間

Anita, just sit back , relax, and enjoy the rest of the day.

Anita，請你坐舒服些、放輕鬆、好好享受今天剩餘的時光。

㊴ on condition that：在……條件之下

I'll let you go home on condition that you finish your reading by 6:00 p.m..

如果你在傍晚六點之前能讀完，我就讓你回家。

㊵ in time：及時，在某期限之內

和準時（on time）有程度上差異

I really hope Sun Farm will pay in time, otherwise we'll have to hold their shipment.

我真希望 Sun Farm 能及時付款，否則我們得要扣貨了。

㊶ thanks very much：多謝

也可說 Thanks so much、Thanks a lot、Many thanks、Appreciate very much

㊷ hold a meeting：主持會議

Jessica started to work on the agenda after Sammi asked her to hold a meeting next Monday.

在 Sammi 要 Jessica 下週一主持會議後，Jessica 就開始準備討論議題。

NOTE

㊸ in an hour：一小時之內

I was supposed to finish the report in an hour.
我應當在一小時內完成報告的。

㊹ do it right：把事情做對、做正確

To improve work quality, we were requested by the management not only to do the right thing but also to do it right from the beginning.
為了改善工作品質，公司管理階層要求我們不但要做對事情，而且還得從開始就把事情做好。

㊺ from now on：由現在開始

From now on, we'll have to rely on ourselves.
從今起，我們一切得靠自己。

㊻ sort this out：解決、弄清楚

sort 是指「整理、分類」，「sort out」表示整理出頭緒或弄清楚

Take it easy Danny. We'll sort this out quickly.
別著急，Danny，我們很快就能弄清楚。

國家圖書館出版品預行編目資料

B2B企業英語會話～業務篇／李純白著.
— 二版. — 臺北市：五南，2018.05
　　　面；　　公分
ISBN 978-957-11-9683-1（平裝）

1.商業英文　2.會話

805.188　　　　　　　　　107004926

1XOE

B2B企業英語會話～業務篇

作　　　者 ― 李純白

發 行 人 ― 楊榮川

總 經 理 ― 楊士清

副總編輯 ― 黃文瓊

主　　　編 ― 朱曉蘋

編　　　輯 ― 吳雨潔　黃懷萱

封面設計 ― 劉好音　謝瑩君

出 版 者 ― 五南圖書出版股份有限公司

地　　　址：106台北市大安區和平東路二段339號4樓

電　　　話：(02)2705-5066　　傳　　　真：(02)2706-6100

網　　　址：http://www.wunan.com.tw

電子郵件：wunan@wunan.com.tw

劃撥帳號：01068953

戶　　　名：五南圖書出版股份有限公司

法律顧問　林勝安律師事務所　林勝安律師

出版日期　2015年10月初版一刷
　　　　　　2018年 5 月二版一刷

定　　　價　新臺幣360元